THE SHELTERED QUARTER

A TALE OF A BOYHOOD IN MECCA

MODERN MIDDLE EAST

LITERATURES IN TRANSLATION

SERIES

Hamza Bogary

The Sheltered Quarter
A Tale of a Boyhood in Mecca

Translated by
Olive Kenny and Jeremy Reed
from the Saudi Arabian novel
Saqifat Al-Safa

Introduction by William Ochsenwald

Center for Middle Eastern Studies
University of Texas at Austin

Library of Congress Catalog Card Number: 91-072518

ISBN 0-292-72752-6

Printed in the United States of America

Cover: Diane Watts

Editor: Annes McCann-Baker

Arabic version of *Saqifa't Al-Safa* published by Dar al-Rifai
1983, Riyadh, Saudi Arabia

Front illustration adapted from Arabic edition cover
by Ahmad al Dieb.

Table of Contents

On the Author

Hamza Mohammad Bogary was born in Mecca, Saudi Arabia, in 1932. After completing his higher studies in Cairo, he worked for several years in Saudi broadcasting, becoming Director General of Broadcasting in 1962. In 1965 he was appointed Deputy Minister of Information, a post he held until 1967, at which time he established his own business. Mr. Bogary was a co-founder of King Abdulaziz University in Jiddah, an institution founded in 1967 by private individuals and turned over to the government in 1971.

Mr. Bogary published both stories and essays in various periodicals. In 1983 he wrote the present novel based on his early observations of life in Mecca, transforming knowledge into art through various devices: a rare sense of humor, a deep empathy, a remarkable understanding of human nature and a universal outlook on life and man. The novel abounds with descriptions of a bygone way of life which has now irreversably disappeared. These qualities give this unusual novel a special importance. It was Mr. Bogary's last tribute to his own culture and to Arabic literature before his death in 1984.

Foreword

Hamza Bogary's *Saqifat Al-Safa*, a fictional work based on authentic personal experience depicting life in Mecca before the advent of oil, is the first translation done by the Project of Translation from Arabic (PROTA) in a new series of works delineating aspects of Arab life in the twentieth century that are no longer extant. Works in preparation by PROTA that fall under this category are:

Hanna Mina's novel, *Fragments of Memory*, on life among the poorest sections of society in northern Syria in the 1920s.

Al-Bashir Ben Slama's novel, *Aisha*, on life in Tunisia at the turn of the twentieth century.

Zayd Mutee' Dammaj's novel, *The Hostage*, on life in Yemen during the rule of the Imams.

Saqifat Al-Safa is, moreover, the fourth novel translated by PROTA to be published. The other three are:

Emile Habiby's, *The Secret Life of Saeed, The Pessoptimist*, 1982, and 2nd. printing by Zed Books, London, 1985.

Sahar Khalifeh's, *Wild Thorns*, Saqi Books, London, 1985.

Muhammad Yusuf al-Qaeed's, *War in the Land of Egypt*, Saqi Books, London, 1986.

Other PROTA translations of novels to be published in the future include:

Ibrahim Nasrallah's, *Prairies of Fever.*

Yasin Rifa'iyyeh's, *The Corridor*

Salma Khadra Jayyusi
Director, PROTA

Acknowledgments

I would like to thank Dr. Mansour al-Hazimi, chairman of the Department of Arabic at King Saud University for drawing my attention to this novel.

As a member of King Saud University Board of Editors for the *Literature of Modern Arabia* (KPI, 1988, University of Texas Press, 1990), a joint endeavour between King Saud University and PROTA, he suggested that we select some excerpts from this novel for the Anthology. A Meccan himself and a man of letters, he was certainly in a position to appreciate the novel's value both as a work of fiction and as a vivid account of Meccan life before the advent of oil. Then, when I, on reading the novel, decided that it should also be translated in its entirety by PROTA, Dr. Hazimi was kind enough to put me in touch with H.E. Shaikh Abd al-Aziz al-Rifa'i, the novel's publisher in Arabic, for which I also thank him very much.

My warm thanks are also due to Shaikh Abd al-Aziz al-Rifa'i himself for his faith and kind words regarding our work in PROTA, as well as for his speedy action in writing to the Bogary family on PROTA's behalf, an action which resulted in an immediate positive response from them.

To the Bogary family goes my deepest appreciation for facilitating our work first by subsidizing the translation of the novel, and then by furnishing us with all the necessary information on the late author's life and on particular aspects of the work itself. Their enduring care for the author's memory and their immense kindness to me have touched me deeply.

When we were preparing the novel, we came across many words and references which needed explanation. Only Saudis could help in this respect. However, there were many words which only Meccans could understand, and even then, there were a few others which only Meccans from the older generation could remember. Such were the differences and the change in life-style that the help of several persons was needed to finalize the full glossary of the book. In this respect, I would like to extend my deep gratitude to Dr. Abdallah Ghadhami, Professor of Arabic at King Abd al-Aziz University for recruiting for me the help of his Meccan colleague at the same university, Dr. Ya'qoub Turkustani, whose meticulous and painstaking explanations of words, usages and references in the first part of the novel were extremely useful. I thank him most heartily. I am also deeply indebted to Dr. Mahmoud E. Siny, Professor of applied linguistics and former director of the Arabic language Institute at King Saud University. Although not a Meccan himself, he was able to enlighten me on the meaning of many words with precision and great scholarly patience. My many thanks go also to Sameer Ashi, a Ph.D. student at the University of Michigan. He comes from a well-known Meccan family whose members used to be pilgrims' guides and lived, during the time which the novel depicts, in the neighbourhood of al-Safa. He was able to enlighten me on several words in the novel.

The translators deserve my deepest thanks. Olive Kenny courageously undertook the difficult task of translating a very unusual text, full of references and unfamiliar words that all needed study and research, and the most vigilant attention on the part of any translator. And Jeremy Reed's task of modifying the translated text was no less strenuous. I thank them both very much.

I was very pleased when Dr. William Ochsenwald, Professor of History at the Virginia Polytechnic Institute and State University wrote to me applauding this "excellent account of a fictional life in Mecca," which he believes "deserves the widest possible readership." Being a historian of modern Hijaz himself, his opinion holds weight, and I want to thank him for this as well as for the cogently written introduction he prepared for this book.

Thanks are also due to Walter Amburst, Ph.D. student of Anthropology at the University of Michigan for his meticulous help in the last stages of preparation of this novel, whether in the typing, or in helping me with the research for the annotations of this book.

S.K.J.

Introduction

The first images that occur to most readers of literature in English when they think about the Arabian Peninsula and the Middle East are oil derricks and camels striding across sand dunes. But these images and visions are far from accurate in describing the true reality of Arabia today (and even more inaccurate in regard to earlier times). This excellent novel, *Saqifat Al-Safa*, not only entertains, it also informs its readers about the Arabia of the first half of the twentieth century in a graphic and fascinating way.

The story is set in Mecca in western Arabia, the city where Prophet Muhammad was born and where he received many of his revelations that constituted the Qur'an (Koran), the holy book of Islam. Because of its religious importance, deriving from the presence of the Ka'ba and the annual worldwide pilgrimage to it, Mecca was central to the Ottomans, who controlled it from the early sixteenth century. The Ottomans provided food and money to the people of Mecca and, in return, the local dynasty of *sharifs* helped provide legitimacy to the Ottoman Turkish dynasty of the House of Osman[1]. During World War I the *sharif*, Husain ibn Ali, who had been appointed in 1908, revolted against the Ottomans, allied himself with the British, and gained control of western Arabia and other areas to the north. However, the Saudi rulers of central and eastern Arabia conquered Mecca, Medina, and Jeddah in the 1920s. After the Saudi conquest of Mecca the pilgrimage resumed. It was of vital economic as well as religious importance. Oil was discovered and first shipped in

1938, but it was only in the 1950s that very large quantities of oil were extracted and that Saudi Arabia gained enormous wealth from petroleum[2].

In this novel, Hamza Bogary brings alive, in a very particular and sympathetic way, the Mecca of those days before oil. Much of his account deals with education, the type of materials studied, the manner employed in teaching them and the very amusing ways in which some students accepted the educational structure and others rejected it. The protagonist, Muhaisin al-Baliy, reads avidly, so much so that he takes to reading at night beside a street lamp, since his home has no light strong enough for reading. Bogary also gives much information on the pilgrimage and the treatment of pilgrims, including a memorable trip to Medina. Other aspects of social history are also touched upon in a very realistic way, including the rivalry of urban neighborhoods, slavery, styles of clothing and their meaning, and public executions.

As Muhaisin is exposed to various aspects of modern technology, such as the photograph and phonograph, Bogary shows how a naive and unsophisticated youth gradually adjusts to their novelty. He also vividly discusses the status of women and the nature of the relationship between men and women, as in his account of the use of a male servant to purchase supplies and of the possible impropriety involved in Muhaisin tutoring a female student.

Much in this account also deals with religion. Muhaisin studies formal religion, and he also experiences many examples of folk or informal religious practices. He tells of Auntie Asma, his mother's friend, who believes in many superstitions and unusual practices. Muhaisin broadens his understanding of religion to reach beneath surface conformism. A great help to him in this and many other ways is Amm Umar, a government employee, an avid reader, and a wise and sophisticated man. It is he who represents the forces of modernity in conservative Mecca, and it is he who guides Muhaisin toward a better self- understanding as well as an appreciation of the world beyond Mecca.

The depth of this novel that derives from its particularity is wonderfully complemented by its treatment of universal themes. Bogary writes of Mecca in a way that reminds the reader of other outstanding works that deal with different parts of the Middle East, such as Kurban Said's Baku and Taha Husayn's Cairo[3]. But he also touches upon character traits and behavior similar to that of Mark Twain's *Tom Sawyer*. Muhaisin, like

Tom, wants to be the center of attention, and he embellishes stories about a funeral so as to gain the interest of the other boys at school. There are charming accounts of boyhood nicknames, touching descriptions of a child's reaction to death, and mischievous incidents such as that of Sufyan and the water container. Muhaisin is frank in his language and vivid in his humor. The author shows Muhaisin's weaknesses, an example being his childish vanity about his early literary ventures, but Bogary ultimately makes Muhaisin a character for whom the reader cares deeply. Muhaisin's irony, his love for his mother, and his growth as an individual and as a teacher, along with many other aspects of his behavior and thoughts, should bring him and his milieu alive to a world audience.

This version of the Arabic original is well annotated and contains an excellent glossary of terms. In light of the extreme scarcity of books in English dealing with Mecca in the twentieth century written by Meccans themselves, this translation is particularly valuable. Perhaps the true-to-life images presented here will begin to replace the old stereotypes with a more sympathetic, human, and individual picture of Mecca, Saudi Arabia, and the Middle East.

William Ochsenwald
Professor of History
Virginia Polytechnic Institute

Endnotes to the Introduction

[1] For a fuller account of Mecca in this period, see William Ochsenwald, *Religion, Society and the State in Arabia: The Hijaz under Ottoman Control, 1840-1908* (Columbus: Ohio State University Press, 1984).

[2] For the history of modern Saudi Arabia, see the forthcoming article, William Ochsenwald, "Arabia: Saudi Arabian History," *Encyclopaedia Britannica*.

[3] Kurban Said, *Ali and Nino* (New York: Random House, 1970); Taha Husayn, the three parts of his *al-Ayyam*, and particularly *The Stream of Days* (London: 1948).

The Sheltered Quarter
A Tale of a Boyhood in Mecca

I

Until then I had never seen a person die. At the time of my father's death, I was a little boy, still unable to discriminate between things, and I was sent to my aged grandmother who could not bear to witness her son's dying. When I returned home the following day, I was told without any explanation that my father had died. Therefore, although I did not suffer over it, my uncle's death was a new experience for me. Most children of that age don't distinguish between a funeral or wedding in their house, being interested only in the transformation that occurs within the household and the freedom they enjoy as a consequence of the break in routine. The assembled guests, the lights, the different kinds of food, and the chance to stay up until late at night, are all greeted as welcome distractions.

At the time I was an indifferent pupil who attended a private school separated from our house by a narrow street. The latter was our hangout during recesses between classes and our playground after school. While he was alive, my uncle had repeatedly impressed upon me that I was a good-for-nothing and that, as my life would amount to nothing, I would end up being a burden to others. By way of a bet, he would point to the expansive white beard on his face, and say, "If you succeed I'll shave off my beard." Then, taking hold of it to emphasize his point, he would tug it gently. Sometimes he would substitute another wager, the import of which would leave me confused and distressed. He would say: "If ever you succeed in anything, come and piss on my grave!" Since I had no clear conception of what a grave looked like, I would try to imagine someone pissing on another's grave. Who were these people, I wondered, who went about pissing on graves, and where did they do it? In my child's mind, as I had never encountered this behavior on my way to the mosque or my grandmother's house, I assumed it happened somewhere far away.

Vexed by my uncle's behavior, I used to wish that something would happen to his beard, that either he would decide to shave it off or that it would fall off by itself. I was curious to know how he would look without it, and, with the cruelty of a child, I would sometimes intentionally set out to annoy him. At other times I wished him dead, so that I could obey his instructions and piss on his grave. Nevertheless, after having these thoughts, the innate goodness of the child would triumph, making me cry bitterly and cling to him, patting his whiskers, afraid lest my thoughts should come true.

II

They laid him out, with his hands folded across his chest, upon a wooden bench which was slightly higher than the one we used for a rooftop bed. A man whose very appearance disquieted me stood facing him. He was tall and wore a faded blue girdle around his waist and tattered shoes of a style now obsolete. The man was dipping his hand into a vessel of warm water, then pouring it on the corpse, all the while reciting in a voice that was incomprehensible to me.

Behind the door stood my mother, her sisters, and many other women whom I did not know, all of them weeping for the dead, and with such intensity that one of them fainted. But the man inside the room paid no attention to them. From time to time he would stop what he was doing, roll up his sleeves, and cry out: "People! Declare that He is One. . .declare that God is One!" At this, the wailing would increase, the children accompanying it with their screams, and I too found myself crying. The occasion seemed so serious that I found myself wanting to do something, but unable to identify what that something was.

For a while I succeeded in stifling my tears, until finally I burst into a kind of loud crying I had never experienced before. Impulsively I darted out through the long passageway where my uncle was being washed, and found myself in the street. There an older boy, with whom I had often fought, immediately picked a quarrel with me. No sooner were we

6

embroiled than he took to punching me on the head and chest with his fists and even butted me with his head. I could do little to defend myself except continue crying. Eventually the mourners came out and formed a long line. Four men carried the bier and placed it on the ground in front of the house. After reciting the *Fatiha* over it, one of them cried in a loud voice: "One of the blessed, God willing," after which the sounds of mourning in the women's quarter increased.

When the procession moved on, I remained standing there, uncertain as to what I should do. Should I join the men or return to the house? After a few minutes, the procession receding into the distance and the wailing becoming fainter, I decided to run after the bier.

Barefoot and bareheaded, I ran until I caught up with the procession. By now the crowd had increased. Shopkeepers, the crowd of men ambling toward the mosque to attend afternoon prayer, and others all shared in carrying my uncle's bier. When we arrived at the mosque, we found we had coincided with another funeral, so prayers were said for both of the deceased.

This was my first experience of praying for the dead, but unhappily it wasn't to be the last. In the days to come I was to have much to do with the dead and funerals. But by that time I had reached puberty and had made a vow that I would help carry every dead person to his final resting place, particularly those who were conveyed to their graves unaccompanied by many mourners.

Outside the mosque the body was quickly passed from hand to hand among those who had joined in the procession. Some of them placed their cloaks over their heads, an action that indicated that they belonged to the family of the deceased. I was surprised to find that I who was probably the closest relative went ignored, although I in turn failed to recognize anyone except a *shaikh* whom I knew to be a relative of my uncle.

The people gathered around the grave contended with each other to help lower the coffin, and I, in my anxious concern not to miss anything, contrived to sit on the edge of the grave and take in the scene that has remained with me to this day. My final memory of the burial, before the grave was covered over with stones, was of my uncle's uncovered face with his long white beard escaping over his chest.

That night I hardly slept at all, although it wasn't grief that kept me awake — for neither I nor anyone else, including my mother, had grieved over him — but rather the memorable events of the day. I was obsessed with the sequence of events from the time my uncle was laid out in the morning and his eyes were closed to the last fleeting glimpse I had of him. All of these things, including the sight of his cane and shoes beside the bed I slept on, left an indelible mark on my subconscious and continued to preoccupy me for years to come. Perhaps it was the unflinching reality of death that concerned me, although at the time I was unable to rationalize my fears.

After the three-day period of mourning was over, I returned to school to find that things had changed for the better. The teacher desisted from beating me for a number of days and instead turned his attention to one of my classmates, whom I had unfairly reported. My fellow pupils persisted in gathering round me each morning to inquire about the funeral, the deceased, the man who washed the dead, and the grave itself. I would invent stories that originated in my childish imagination and would add to these my grandmother's tales about the black dog which had barked for three consecutive days before my uncle's death. Fortunately I was skillful enough to alter these improvised stories with each new telling so that my audience never grew bored. But in time the novelty of the story I had lived through lost its attraction, and I ceased to enjoy the privilege of being the center of attention.

III

I don't remember how old I was at the time of these events, any more that I can recall my present age. I've always looked younger than I am, something I attribute to my having been born prematurely and not having completed my fetal development. I was born on Arafa Day,[1] and the undulating motion of the camel that conveyed my mother to the pilgrimage probably had something to do with my untimely birth. Prior to the school I was attending at the time of my uncle's death, I had been educated in two other institutions. The first of these was a *kuttab*, a school for girls, to which I was sent to learn my letters and from which I was removed after a few months after facetiously informing my mother that all I had learned to date was the rhymed list of the alphabet. She struck me for my backwardness and was amazed that I had not progressed to *al-Fatiha*. Although I was soon able to memorize the latter, after my removal to a boy's elementary school, I have never forgotten the rhymed list of the

8

alphabet, and can repeat it today in the same manner as I did more than sixty years ago.

After *al-Fatiha* I came to master the alphabet, or at least I was able to differentiate between *ba* and *ta²*· although it took me a long time to remember *za* as in the word *zaby* (gazelle). I soon realized that this omission could be accounted for by the absence of gazelles in the surrounding area and the lack of somebody capable of describing one to me. However, I circumvented the issue by slurring the letter in a way that the teacher could not detect, and whenever a word containing that sound cropped up, I adopted a natural lisp. The strange thing was that I remembered the way I had invented to articulate the sound, but not the way it was supposed to be pronounced.

From the alphabet, we progressed quickly to the story of the young billy goat who muddied the water for the lion and the crow who imitated the owl. We worked under the teacher's threat that school would not break up that summer until we had finished reading the five selected stories and had irrevocably mastered the alphabet.

At the end of the year which preceded my entry into the National Preparatory School, we celebrated our having mastered the alphabet, with an awe-inspiring ceremony. Pieces of red candy made from sugar and flour and called *batasa* were distributed to each pupil. We then filed through the school door into the narrow alley and on to the neighboring *bazan* in a procession that I still remember whenever I see anyone wearing an academic gown of the kind that has become popular these days.

That last year of my elementary school education proved to be decisive to my eventual academic career, and it was then that I was introduced to the *Rasheeda*³ Book, which I pronounced *Khashabiya* Book, despite the evident difference in pronunciation, for a reason that is still obscure to me.

When I graduated to the Preparatory School the same year that my uncle died, I soon discovered the difference between the *kuttab* and the school. The first was characterized by a single room, while the latter had three rooms and a courtyard! Here to my surprise there was an extravagant increase in teaching staff of one hundred percent over the *kuttab*, since there were two teachers instead of one! It followed that one of the three classes had to be supervised by the head boy of the class. The system subscribed to was roughly as follows: during the first period the two teachers were allocated to the second- and third-year classes, leaving the first-year class under the jurisdiction of the head boy, while in the second

9

period one of the teachers took the first-year class, leaving the deserted class to be instructed by the head boy, and so on. During a crisis, when for example we were visited by wealthy pilgrims, whose intention it was to make donations to the school, one of the senior third-year students was assigned to our class as a teacher.

Our headmaster, *Shaikh* Ishaq, was one of the two teachers. He would largely confine himself to the third-year class, as visitors to the school lingered there, asking the students difficult questions about reciting the Quran. In order for the visit to be successful, the *shaikh* would see to it that the questions were directed to the most intelligent pupils.

IV

Most of the boys had names which derived from the word 'Abd; some were called after the prophet Muhammad (or used a derivative of his name);[4] others had the names of the angels or the godly. But at school we lost these pious derivations and were known simply as "the tall one," *al-Haballo* or "dunce," "blue eyes," and so on. Worse still, in times of anger the nickname would be distorted to something like "Blue-eyed enemy of the Muslims," which in time would simply become "Enemy of the Muslims." Likewise, Ahmad al-Haballo would keep his nickname until we moved on to a private school where he earned the title of *al-Duhul.*[5] It never occurred to me at the time that the name would stick to Ahmad for life, and when he died recently I discovered that his name had been entered on a payroll in a clothing factory in Mecca as Ahmad al-Duhul, janitor. To each of these names we attached a special significance, and they became a shared code among us, except for the troubling nickname given to one of our friends whose real name was Sufyan. *Shaikh* Ishaq called him "the unlawful offspring," and, since the boys gradually formulated a substitute for this derogation, his name became a dirty word as far as canonical law is concerned.

It wasn't that Sufyan didn't work hard for his nickname; he cultivated it assiduously at school and during periods of recess. We even imagined him enacting the role at home, eventually taking it with him into sleep.

He would come to school with his pockets full of a small round fruit called *nabaq*, or lotus fruit, which he would proceed to gobble in class. When we weren't looking, he would pelt us with the stones, even daring

10

to aim at the teacher. No one ever dared inform on him, despite the fact that the whole class would receive the strap when the teacher was unable to uncover the true culprit. Between classes it was not uncommon for Sufyan to test the strength of the writing slates by knocking one against the other until one split, and then to leave the pieces lying on the floor in the middle of the room. Provoking others was a sport he cultivated to a fine art. Concealed in a corner, he would lie in wait until a boy came hurrying past and then stick his foot out and trip the boy. A fight would immediately ensue, and each day he contrived to experiment with a new trick.

Shaikh Ishaq came to school wearing a white robe and white jacket, complemented by a grey cloak and turban. After folding his cloak, he would place it in a small chest where he kept chalks of various colors, writing tools and his cane; this was a practice he repeated each day. No one will ever know how Sufyan sneaked to the box and managed to flip a match at the cloak, leaving a burn hole the size of a Majidi *riyal.* And although he wasn't detected in the act, we suspected that he was responsible. As a consequence he was expelled from school, but later readmitted due to his father's mediation with *Shaikh* Ishaq.

More than once he was to be observed standing behind the *Shaikh,* tying the fringes of the Shaik's turban cloth into a large knot so that the boys would laugh at him as he went along. Once as a joke Sufyan brought a long rope and attached a stone to one end of it and a clothespin to the other, fastened it to the hem of the *shaikh's* robe, and skedaddled. The *shaikh,* unaware, dragged the stone along making a strange noise. Despite all his tricks, Sufyan stayed on at school until the third year, when the big mishap occurred.

In the way that people remember The Year of the Elephant[6] (the elephant of the famous *Sherif),* The Year of the Big Flood[7] and The Year of Mercy[8] (in which so many died), I, had I been asked, would have called that particular year The Year of the *Zeer.* The *zeer* was a huge earthen vessel capable of holding twenty gallons by today's measurements. It was usually filled in the afternoon, so that the water could cool overnight for drinking purposes the next day. A cup, fastened to the handle by a lightly padlocked chain, was placed to accommodate our needs. Although this cup was stolen on a number of occasions and the lock broken, it didn't warrant a serious inquiry. But what follows is of a more extreme nature.

Since my memory fails me, I got the details of the story from trustworthy members of our former school, who were still alive. Apparently, one

11

morning *Shaikh* Ishaq, on his arrival at the school courtyard, was shocked to find the zeer removed from its customary place. For some moments he stood staring in a state of disbelief at the damp spot left by the absent zeer. Unable to find a satisfactory solution to the enigma, he paced restlessly from one schoolroom to another in the hope of solving the mystery. Unable to satisfy himself as to a plausible explanation, he went and stood out in the street. He was even sufficiently troubled to lead some people that were passing by to the spot in the courtyard formerly occupied by the zeer. Puzzled by this irrational behavior and mostly unaware that a zeer had occupied the courtyard, they not unnaturally asked for an explanation. In answer to their questions the *Shaikh* made it abundantly clear that the missing article had been in its proper place on the previous evening. And when the pupils began arriving, he asked each in turn: "Have you seen the zeer?" He responded to each negative answer by delivering two sharp cane blows on the palm of the hand. Having done with this, he assembled the school in the courtyard and asked us collectively: "Have you seen the zeer?" As we all denied knowledge of its whereabouts, he was forced to rethink the issue, and decided to send the entire school home, while he remained behind with the other teachers. After a period of studied thought, the *Shaikh* said emphatically: "Of course, it could only be one person, Sufyan the son of a ------, employing the dirty word that had become common usage among the boys. When the other teacher was at pains to point out that the zeer was much too large for Sufyan to lift, his reply was that the devil had ways of maneuvering that would never cross the mind of anyone but Sufyan, and of that he was convinced.

The school remained closed for two days, during which time several meetings were held, the last of these taking place at Sufyan's house, where his father doubted his son's guilt in the matter. His suggestion was that everyone should contribute toward purchasing a replacement, and that he himself should be the first contributor. After careful thought *Shaikh* Ishaq agreed to the proposal on the condition that Sufyan should never be allowed to return to school. When the father naturally objected to the decision and threatened to withdraw his donation, the majority tried to persuade the *Shaikh* to change his mind. The latter stuck to his guns, and the meeting was adjourned without a satisfactory resolution.

That day after evening prayer the notables of the quarter met in the local mosque to discuss the matter as well as the inconvenience of having their children at home for two days. Deciding to sacrifice Sufyan, they collected

12

the required sum and handed it over to the *shaikh,* who duly set out the next morning for the potter's. He returned in a jubilant mood, followed by a Nubian porter carrying the replacement zeer on his head. It appeared to be a little larger and quite plainly whiter than its predecessor.

Despite the irrevocable decision of the quarter and its notables, there were those who continued to intercede for Sufyan; but their mediation was to no avail. And that wasn't all: the *Shaikh* even went so far as to pronounce that Sufyan would eventually come to the same end as one of the two prison companions of Joseph the Righteous. As he refused to elaborate on this statement, its meaning invited diverse speculation.

It wasn't until much later that I was able to clear up the points that had puzzled me at the time, and this only by meeting the accused and ascertaining from him his part in the affair. He confessed to me that he had taken a large stone into school that day and left it there until the afternoon. He had then scaled the wall and, by throwing the stone at the zeer, succeeded in splitting it in two. By repeating the action, he was able to break the vessel into four pieces and place the segments on top of the wall. Then, climbing out at sunset, he had removed the fragments to the site of a ruin near the school. Those fragments, he added, had remained there for several years before he eventually lost track of them.

V

Despite all that Sufyan had done and would continue to do in the coming years, I did not share in the general pleasure aroused by his expulsion. There was something that drew me to him, a kind of secret admiration. Whatever biased interpretation may be put on such an attachment by our contemporaries, both the mischievous and the meek among them, facts remain facts, and to me Sufyan remained a source of excitement and an initiator of great discoveries.

Just as the Portuguese voyager Magellan is remembered today for his exploits at sea, so Sufyan, the Meccan, deserves more than anyone else to be remembered for his exploits upon the land. Wasn't it he who made me aware that the world was not comprised of that narrow street I crossed: that confined area between two mountains — Abu Qubais and the Seven Girls — with the even narrower alleys branching off it, all of them coming to a dead end on the right or left, smack up against one or the other of the mountains?

Wasn't it Sufyan who conducted me for the first time through the dark Saqifa of al-Safa into the wide world that terminated after several hours' walking to the Jinn's Haunt, from where we passed by the thieves' dens and the ascent to Abu Lahab. It didn't matter that I spent a feverish night as a consequence of walking so long exposed to the midday sun, or that my feet were ready to give out near the end of the trip, for the pleasure lay in the discovery and the delight at returning home after enduring so many discomforts. My only reservation about our first reconnaissance journey had to do with the events that occurred after our reaching Jinn's Haunt, the highest point in Mecca. I could not fathom what sort of *jinn* were imprisoned there, and Sufyan suggested we adjourn to a coffee house. In view of our young age, the owner refused us entry, but with characteristic cunning Sufyan returned and spoke to the owner's servant boy, telling him that our mother was sitting on a mountainside road behind the coffee house, and, being unable as a woman to enter this place, she required that her sons bring her water and tea. The request was agreed to, Sufyan paid for the tea, and together we enjoyed our refreshments at a distance from the coffeehouse.

When we were ready to commence our return journey, he took the pot and little glasses and broke them to smithereens and, pulling me by the hand, continued on his way. To my way of thinking this sort of behavior was unnecessary, but...

After that, and perhaps for the best, days passed by without my seeing him. Then he returned, excited by new discoveries, but they were less glamorous and did not arouse the old admiration I had felt after the day of the Jinn's Haunt. However, there was one Friday I shall never forget. He rapped at our door in midmorning and told me he wished to show me something the like of which I had never seen before. I followed him, and, after a few minutes' walk, he veered to the left, taking me through the back door of a large building called al-Hameediya, which was guarded at the front and rear by two soldiers armed to the teeth. Inside the hall, Sufyan pointed to framed pictures, each of which bore the individual's name. I didn't find his actions entertaining, even when he singled out a series of pictures representing the infamous of Mecca, those who might be designated "The Outlaws of the Fourteenth Century."[10] As I complained of still not having seen anything unexpected, Sufyan told me to wait a while, and together we sat on the stairs leading to the upper floor. We remained here until a growing hubbub had him lead me to the balcony overlooking the mosque and the front gate of the building. There, indeed, I saw something I had never witnessed before. In the direct line of my vision I saw a man's head cut off by a sword. Had I been standing on sand, my feet would have sunk into the ground, as they say in stories. However, as I was standing on a solid surface, they shook uncontrollably until I fainted. And from that day on I became convinced of what was said about Sufyan...

Fortunately, my mother wasn't aware of what had happened and had no occasion to find out. I simply told her that I'd suffered a spell of dizziness accompanied by sickness and that already I was feeling better, so there was no cause for alarm. She contented herself with shaking her head, a mannerism she employed whenever she felt powerless to comment on a situation or event. If I was someone prone to exaggeration, I would doubtless elaborate on the dreams that plagued me after the bloody event of that Friday, but nothing of the kind happened to me. The only dream I had that night was about Sufyan, and in it, it was he who vomited, not I. I had regained my composure by the Saturday, and two days elapsed without my coming to any final decision about my relationship with Sufyan.

All I assured myself was that I would undertake no future escapades with him unless I was told of our destination, and, if this called for a modification of our friendship, then it also saved me from what might have been excruciating ordeals. We still met from time to time in the open space in front of my house, and he would tell me of some of his exploits. Now that he no longer had to attend school, his time was his own, and he devoted a part of it to beating up every boy in the class he had belonged to, who had shown pleasure at his misfortune. He beat them all up and often in front of my eyes. Catching hold of one or two of them, he dealt out to them what they had never received in their lives: punches, kicks, butts, and so on. I was nonplussed. Would I in time get my share like the rest of them? Or was Sufyan going to take my continuing friendship into account and spare me.

The matter was resolved in a way I had not anticipated. For a reason unknown to me, Sufyan had decided to put off beating up *Amm* Umar's son until the last. This decision showed both wisdom and foresight, since he spent the night subsequent to assaulting *Amm* Umar's son in the police station in al-Safa, where Murad Effendi, the officer on duty, spat on him and kicked him. He was then committed to a dark room. It was painful to see Sufyan led out, his hands tied with rope, pursued by a crowd of boys, including two of the quarter's idiots, all cheering as if the occasion were a wedding. When he returned the next day through the *Saqifa* of al-Safa, dark even in the daytime, he kept to the shadows and had lost his former audacity. Had I seen him that day I would have understood the meaning of the saying "So and so has lost his sting." He had been a scorpion possessed of a deadly sting, but it had disappeared overnight. He wasn't to recover it for several years, and then only when he became a stonemason, heading a team of animals carrying stones, and curbing them as though he were leading a victorious army replete with warriors and weapons.

VI

"You have been orphaned twice, my son," said Auntie Asma, beating her breast. "Most people are orphaned only once. Under what unlucky star were you born, my child?"

Her voice screeched like an owl's. Although I did not feel orphaned until I said farewell to my mother almost twenty years later, Auntie Asma succeeded in communicating to me that my lot was an unfortunate one.

My mother and I were paying a visit to her, for she was an old friend and the quarter's female doctor, who was renowned for treating gripes and fevers in a decisive way. If one was taken ill with pleurisy, her method was to cauterize the feet and sides. No one questioned her good- heartedness and the love of people which made her so instrumental in dispelling their problems. It was therefore for a variety of reasons that Mother looked to her for guidance, and also because she was adept at reading fortunes from seashells. It was she who read in the sea-shells that Mother would drown twice. In symbolic terms that meant that she would marry twice and lose both husbands. This was after my mother had been divorced by her first husband, Irfan Bey. Auntie Asma grew to assume a role of great influence in our lives and in mine particularly, for after my uncle's death, she became the family consultant. My mother took to visiting her at least once a week in order to tell her of recent events or to have Auntie Asma interpret her dreams. She would also ask for counsel about my affairs, my school, my future, and my prospective employment.

Despite her laments that I had been orphaned twice, my condition improved after my uncle's death, the latter also being my mother's third husband. The first intimation of the tide having changed for the better was my being moved from the small roof bed to one of the two main beds. I took my uncle's place beside my mother and delighted in listening to her stories about jinns and giants, and knights who rescued maidens by carrying them off on the backs of chargers who flew above the clouds. And, while she spoke, her soft hand toyed gently with my thick black hair, until I fell blissfully asleep and dreamed of events issuing from the day and from the nighttime's narratives.

Gradually, I came to learn a great deal from Mother, about life in general and about her first husband, Irfan Bey, who rode a horse. He was a lawyer in his day who, according to her, "had deservedly filled his cloak" with good. No matter her devotion to him, he had divorced her in the end because, as she liked to put it, he was a mule. That is, he was unable to sire children and attempted to attach the blame to my mother's infertility.

When I enquired how she could be certain about this, she replied that she had consulted two women soothsayers of the quarter, and had in addition worn an amulet guaranteed to promote fertility. And, to support this claim, there had also been the incident of the soothsayer who had dreamed that Mother would have a number of sons. As I was her only son, she interpreted this dream in the light of her possibly marrying or "drowning" for a third time — a marriage that would result in children. She would give me a strange look as if to say "What's hidden in time is even better." Although, despite the prediction, another marriage was never realized, she conducted herself right up until the time of her death as if she were imminently expecting the auspicious newcomer with whom she would end her days.

In the course of those rooftop evenings, I learned that her second husband, my father, had been a scholar who wore a turban and *jubba*. She had discovered nothing about him to take exception to except that he was too old and was undoubtedly a contemporary of her father. She was obliged to marry him after Irfan Bey because a woman could not live without "the odor of a man," as she expressed it. Their conjugal life was a short one. He died a few years after the marriage, leaving her the house we lived in and an only child, me. It would seem to be this theory of "the odor of a man" that induced her to marry my father's brother. He had nothing to distinguish him apart from this "odor." He was on a lower social scale than my father. He wasn't a scholar wearing a *jubba* but a butcher in a robe belted at the waist, the common lot of all those who were not scholars.

17

VII

As soon as the necessary legal period after my uncle's death had expired,[11] during which she had been prohited from going out or traveling, my mother decided to take me on a visit to Medina and the Prophet's shrine. As usual, my mother consulted Auntie Asma, who decided to accompany us on the journey. As camels were the only accommodative form of transport, Auntie Asma decided to locate a family in our quarter which was intent on visiting the holy shrine, and append our camel to their caravan. Our first inquiry met with success, and we planned to join a large family intent on travelling in a caravan of five camels; but for some inexplicable reason Auntie Asma had by this time lost interest in the scheme. Her search started all over again until she located another caravan whose time of departure coincided with her own. Since both Auntie Asma and my mother conformed to the traditions and customs of the time, Auntie Asma, in accordance with custom, brought a man to our house on the day we were due to depart. At first I couldn't make out what he was supposed to do, particularly as he withdrew to one of the remoter rooms in the house. After he had settled down and accepted tea, he began chanting, while Auntie Asma directed her movements between the window overlooking the street and the long corridor that terminated in the room in which the man was chanting. As I grew accustomed to it, the voice appeared more pleasing, and I was able to recognize the words he was chanting, all of which either related to our anticipated voyage to Medina or were prayers invoking peace on the Prophet. When I eventually found the courage, I asked Auntie Asma to explain the relationship between her frequent visits to the window and the room in which this stranger to the house was chanting. Those familiar with the customs of the time will know that the ceremonial chanter was the *muzahhid*, the resonance of whose voice induced people to discredit earthly things and generated in them a longing to visit Medina. Auntie Asma's frequent alternations between the window and the corridor were to ensure that no one who disapproved of such unorthodox religious practices would hear the *muzahhid's* melodious voice.

Later, on coming of age, I was to ask God forgiveness for the many unorthodox religious practices I had followed while under the guidance of my mother and Auntie Asma. But I have never forgotten, and never will, and I hope to be forgiven for this, the beauty of the *muzahhid's* voice as he chanted — "God's prayers and peace be on you, Prophet."

18

That afternoon our camel driver, Atiyya, led out our camel, while I sat in the *shugduf* between the two women. Our first few anxious moments were spent earnestly praying against the devil, for we were unaccustomed to the dizzy heights of a camel's back and expected at any moment to fall. But after traveling for a short distance, we grew calmer; our camel was even-tempered and we appeared to be in no immediate danger. Our feeling of confidence was enhanced when we caught sight of the rest of the caravan on the outskirts of Mecca. What I hadn't counted on was that the *muzahhid* would be waiting for us there, oblivious to possible observation, bidding us farewell with melodious chants and wishing the pilgrims acceptance by God and His Prophet.

Although I was to journey often through those same plains and hills, the smell of the caravan at twilight was never sweeter to me than during those initial twelve days of travel between Mecca and Medina. Suhail and I, who were the only two boys undertaking the journey, would romp around behind the camels before night fell and we were constrained to take our places in the *shugduf.* Trailing the camels, running through the dry grasses, and observing flying locusts was to us an experience comparable to the best adventures of youth. Of course, we all suffered the occupational hazards of caravan travel, the inescapable mosquito bites, bruises on our sides from sleeping on the backs of camels, but these were small things to pilgrims on their way to visit the best of all mankind.

During the course of the journey Auntie Asma was to tell me about the "Terror of the Night." It was he who would intercept caravans at nightfall and, on the pretext of offering friendly advice to the drivers, would lead them astray and ultimately to their death. A characteristic decoy of his was to set up illusory cafes in the desert stretches, the lights of which would attract the drivers in the same way as a lost bedouin will head towards a mirage in the expectation of finding water. The caravans would never be seen again, and nothing survived of the people, camels, and goods they were conveying.

Auntie Asma was full of stories about those who had met their deaths at the hands of the notorious "Terror of the Night." As a safeguard, she remained awake while the caravan was in motion, ready to warn the drivers, lest they be lured astray and all of us lost.

It must have been when we were between al-Safra and the Nar Valley that, one evening, I heard Auntie Asma's protracted, frantic screams ring through the last vestiges of the night. "The Terror of the Night! The Terror of the Night! Don't be misled by him, he comes to lie!" Startled out of sleep, I almost jumped off the camel in fright. Without effect my mother and the camel driver tried to calm her down, but all the while she continued screaming "The Terror of the Night." And what a commotion! She continued until the drivers brought the caravan to a halt, made our camel kneel, took the trembling Auntie Asma down, and poured a jug of water over her head. Having regained her composure, she was then in a state to listen to them and learn that her imagined "Terror of the Night" was only the figure of the cafe owner where we had put up the previous night. He had pursued us on a camel after discovering that one of our party had left a blanket on a chair in the cafe. Anxious, lest on our discovery of the missing item we had suspected that it was he who had stolen it, he had followed us to return it to its rightful owner.

After that Auntie Asma's obsession with the "Terror of the Night" diminished, but her imagination proved irrepressibly fertile in the collection of exciting narratives she was to have in store for me.

VIII

We had been traveling for eight nights, and, after eight stations, our caravan arrived at Badr.[12] No one anticipated any improbable occurrence that evening, and, arriving just before sunset, the camels were made to kneel by one of the shacks along the road, mats were spread on the sand, and preparations for our meal began as usual. Our supper consisted of a kind of *tharid* made of dry bread we had carried with us from Mecca, cooked with a small quantity of dry meat and water. After supper, Auntie Asma untied her clothes bundle, took out a few requirements, and then sat alone at a distance from the hut. There she began her cosmetic ritual, first of all combing her hair, and then proceeding to rub coconut oil mixed with herbs on it. Satisfied with the remedial arrangements for her hair, she then placed a triangular strip of white cloth over it, and tied the two attached strings at the back of her head. This white cloth was called a *shanbar*. She then wrapped her braid in a handkerchief called a *mahrama* and covered her head with a white shawl with embroidered ends called a *mudawwara*. And, as a final act of embellishment she penciled her eyebrows and applied *kohl* eye-liner to her eyelids. One would have thought she was making herself up for a wedding.

When the others were preparing to retire for the night, Auntie Asma led me by the hand toward the desert. When we were sufficiently far away from the encampment, she sat down on a small dune and motioned me to take a place next to her. As the night deepened, she began those gestures which were to develop into a quiet dance, and then by degrees into a frenzied one. It seemed to me that she was dancing to a tune coming to us from far away, a drum or tambourine beat. She continued whirling while I sat terrified on the sand, wondering whether Auntie Asma had lost her mind, or whether I was dreaming. Only after she was exhausted, and the night was waning, did she return to her place and rest. Taking my hand, she walked me back to the caravan. Mother showed no surprise at our late arrival, seeing the perspiration that beaded Auntie Asma. I was curious to know at once the nature of this dance, but my mother signaled to me to wait until Auntie Asma had gone to sleep; then she would explain all to me. She asked me first of all whether I had heard drums, to which I replied that I had heard reverberant noises whose source I couldn't identify. In reply she explained to me that these notes came from the drums of the warriors at Badr, martyrs who had fallen in that battle, and that, at certain times of the year when the moon is full, their drums are heard again sounding in the desert. According to my mother, Auntie Asma was one of the few who knew when and where to intersect with this phenomenon. And this explained why she had refused to take the first caravan, for its arrival at Badr would have failed to coincide with the return of the martyred drummers. She then requested that I keep the incident secret, as the more orthodox expressed misgivings about the existence of those drums and had people refrain from dancing to their beat.

I can't properly recall now whether my reactions to what I had heard were negative or positive. But I did continue to give the matter thought until I was considerably older and had come to read the ode of Dhu al-Rumma,[13] that speaks of jinn playing tunes in the desert: "The soft humming of the jinn by night on the desert fringes." Poor deluded Dhu al-Rumma and Auntie Asma; they knew nothing of the movement of sand in the desert, and the undulating drifts that the wind mapped out at night.

After the fevered pitch of her dance, Auntie Asma grew calm. She ceased to express anxiety, and her face showed the same serene countenance as those of the other women who, in the days to come, would sit in the circle of the *zar* held in our house in Mecca. I was to see that same expression later on in the faces of young European women and men, whom I saw on weekends, New Years, weddings, and whenever they grew excited by the beat of drums and flute. If I had wished to discourage those young people, I could have done so by informing them that the primitive African tribes I had met in the course of my travels arrived at the same psychological state of gratification after a night of dancing to rhythmic drums — and to songs that were not so very different from those of the Badr or the Latin Quarter. Man is probably as much a rhythmic musical animal as he is a thinking one.

Not that Auntie Asma's new-found serenity stopped her from telling her customary exciting stories, or from making decisions that had the air of being sudden, but which were in fact studied with care. It was for my benefit alone that she told the story of the people of al-Furaish. "Al-Furaish,"[14] she explained, "is a village situated between al-Musaijeed and Abyar Ali. And today the Meccans still refer to someone who overcharges as being from al-Furaish, a custom that derives from these people being the last highway robbers on the road to Medina. So even if the pilgrims had escaped the brigands at Mastura or al-Safra, they still had to confront those of al-Furaish." Although I never attributed lies to Auntie Asma, I did wonder at her telling me about the bedouin whose head she had crushed, many years ago, against the bottom half of the tent pole, after she had caught him scouting while they were camping at al-Furaish. She had hit him impulsively on the head with the nearest object at hand, a picture that had me imagine her brawny-armed, although nothing in her appearance suggested the likelihood of such strength.

Her last decision before our entry into Medina, the City of Light, after having completed the detailed proceedings required by the police at the Anbariyya Gate, was to order the camel driver to pull our camel out of the caravan and to go in the opposite direction from the others. On reaching the area to the south of the Prophet's Mosque, we realized the wisdom of that move. Having ordered the camel driver to stop, she untied a knot in her head shawl and took out a folded letter. Then, alighting from the camel, she proceeded to saunter into the vestibule of a large palace. She returned for us shortly, and it was there that we took up residence for our stay in Medina.

Adopting my usual method of gesturing with my finger when I wanted to inquire about something I didn't understand, I asked my mother to explain the incident. I learned that Auntie Asma, with characteristic foresight, had visited a notable of our quarter, a property owner in Medina, to ask of him permission for us to use one of his houses during our sojourn. As his properties stood empty for most of the year, being in demand only at the time of religious festivals, he readily consented to her request and provided her with a letter to present to the guard at the house. He had granted us the use of the upper sitting room overlooking the date grove, the waterwheel, and small fountain. All of these were new discoveries for me. I had never before seen a fountain, nor heard of a waterwheel. I knew of the latter only through the story of "The Peacock that Stood Beside the Waterwheel" in the Rasheeda Reader. For the record, it was this visit which had generated my infatuation with Medina and resolutely determined me to go there each year once I gained my independence.

On the last day of our sojourn, after paying the farewell visit to the holy shrine together with a large number of fellow pilgrims, Auntie Asma fainted, or at least that is what I presumed at the time. Her cloaked body went down in front of the railing surrounding the holy shrine. Her sudden fall shook the grillwork that protected the tomb and caused an uproar that soon had worshippers and the mosque guards in attendance. Auntie Asma just lay there, her hands clasped to the railing, while those nearest to her tried to lift her up. Throughout the incident, I found myself repeating the *hawqala*: "There is no power or might except in God," and reciting the Fatiha over and over, asking God inwardly not to let Auntie Asma die here, far from her home and the rest of her family.

When at last she attempted to stand, I thanked God for granting my supplications and for protecting us from a possible tragedy. I was not aware at the time that what had taken place was nothing more than dramatics on the part of Auntie Asma. She had conceived of staging a fainting fit in order to come into contact with the railing surrounding the holy tomb. She herself told me later that she was renowned for collapsing there and that she could never contemplate returning to Mecca without first resting her hand on that green grill.

IX

Mother decided to terminate the services of Misfir, who carried water to our house in two tin cans suspended on either side of his shoulders by a bamboo rod. Her excuse for this decision was that it had become improper for Misfir, as a young man, to call on an unattended widow. His replacement was *Amm* Basheer, an elderly Nubian, who conveyed the water in a skin rather than in tin cans. But, in depriving herself of Misfir's services, Mother had perhaps not taken into account the diverse duties he had undertaken for her. It was he who carried Mother's wooden tray of loaves to the public oven for baking and who killed the rooster or hen for the preparation of a special meal. It was Misfir who cleaned the carpets and bed covers during the last ten days of Ramadan and who took for himself, or for other deserving people, the alms given out at the breaking of the fast. In addition, he used to grind the grain, transport heavy objects inside the house, and even buy provisions from the local grocer and butcher. Misfir's dismissal meant that some of his responsibilities now devolved to me. *Amm* Basheer was not only old, but also half blind, and lacked the strength for these duties. He carried no knife in his belt with which to kill a chicken or even an ant, and belonged to a group of water carriers who sat every afternoon on what was known in our quarter as the Bench of the Slaves, all of these men having been freed only after they grew too old and feeble for service.

With *Amm* Basheer joining our household, my curiosity was directed toward that bench and its associations. The troop of water carriers had their own *Shaikh,* and the bench was the strict province of members of their trade. They spoke an African language which was meaningless to me and remembered a past that had its origin in the roots of a village on the Black Continent. Each of them could remember a series of masters who had bought or sold him for one particular reason or another. Some of the freed slaves could even recall a son or daughter who one day was sold away and vanished without trace. And they all shared in common the facility to recount tales, some sad and some funny, about their former experiences.

I also discovered that the bench had its own code of conduct, and that those who violated the rules were accordingly punished. From what I could determine, most of these offenses were directly related to behavior pertaining to the well from which they drew water. If one of them pushed out of turn or made offensive remarks, he was tried after the noonday prayers at the bench. There the *shaikh* sat surrounded by the elders, while the accused was made to squat. The accusation would be made, and witnesses brought in to testify. The accused would then be asked to confess, invariably receiving, by way of punishment, a flogging with the leather belt that the *shaikh* wore around his chest. Stretched out on the ground, the victim would receive no more than three lenient strokes, unless of course the plaintiff pardoned the defendant, or unless some busybody threw a green bunch of clover or leek into the middle of the circle. This was a sign for the court to adjourn and for the injured party to be reprieved, much to the consternation of the presiding *shaikh,* who boiled with anger at the person who had interrupted the proceedings. This type of intervention usually came about at the hands of a local trouble-maker like Sufyan.

As to discovering the symbolic meaning of the green bunch being thrown into the circle, I was never able to discover anyone sufficiently well informed to explain the principle to me. It may have had some remote connection with the olive branch in the biblical story of the flood.

The frequency of my return to that bench gave me access to the stories told, most of which concerned the masters who had sold or freed their slaves. I learned that masters often conducted illicit sexual relations with their slave women, regarding the latter as their property, and, when the girl became pregnant, would marry her off to one of their household slaves so as to avoid acknowledging their paternity, and what would have been the child's right to an inheritance. *Amm* Basheer was full of such stories. He would speak of Mahsoun, Said, and others, who were, in truth, the sons of their rich masters, and not their slaves. Many tales circulated in connection with the women of their masters' households, and they were invariably unpleasant. I would prefer to think that they were the product of *Amm* Basheer's imagination, otherwise my confidence in the moral conduct of those days would be no better than my view of today's morality.

X

"May God strike them down... May God strike them down," reiterated Auntie Asma as she bent over and applied a watering can to the bed of aromatic plants she had arranged beside the roof-top bed on her house couched in the curve of Abu Qubais. It was shortly before sunset, and I was out on an errand for my mother who had asked me to take a bundle of brightly colored strips of cloth to Auntie Asma with the request that she make her some suitable underclothes to wear at the beginning of Shaaban, the month preceding Ramadan. "May God strike them down... May God strike them down," Auntie Asma repeated over and over again, obliging me to inquire about those on whom she was invoking evil. "Riflemen," she replied.

25

"Which riflemen do you mean, Auntie Asma?" I asked. "The ones who kill dogs," she said. "But which dogs are you referring to, and what have you to do with it?" I asked.

"The street dogs," she said, emphatically. "They claim they are mad and shoot them. But if God wanted dogs to die, why did He create them?" That statement has remained fresh in my mind for more than half a century. It occurs to me unconsciously and not necessarily in connection with the subject of dogs. I use it as an axiom to appease those whose rage is directed at some sectors of society or some conditions in general, reminding them that if God had wished to eliminate them, then why would He have created them?

It appears that Auntie Asma was gifted with foresight. To date no one has been able to exterminate the dogs, even though they have been working at it for half a century. This supports her theory of divine providence, despite the fact that Asian people have taken to eating dogs, if we are to believe what we hear.

Although the matter concerning dogs may have been an insignificant one, I continued to think of it for a long time, particularly in relation to the role played by dogs in ancient and modern history. If dogs became extinct, how could our generation understand God's words: "So the likeness of him is as the likeness of a dog; if thou attackest it, it lolls its tongue out, or if thou leavest it it lolls its tongue out."[15] And without this knowledge, how could our youth presume to understand our famous poet's comparison in a line addressed to the Caliph: "You are like the dog in your loyalty to friends." They will be left with the second hemistich: "And like the billy goat in fighting calamities."[16] Similarly the loss of the goat would deprive Arabic poetry of a line which has served to inflame the imagination of countless generations of readers.

The loss of such creatures would also lead to the impoverishment of our folklore, for dogs bark and donkeys bray when a devil passes through our quarter, and the proverb "the caravan proceeds though the dogs bark at it" would become redundant. Nor could we refer to someone as being "more unclean than a dog's tail," and gone too would be the ritual of washing a vessel seven times and once with earth.[17] We would also lose the traditional story of the Israelite who went to paradise because he filled his slipper with water and gave a dog a drink.

But to return to Auntie Asma, I feel sure that her concern for the welfare of dogs originated from human kindness. She belonged to a pre-psychological age, one which looked neither for motives of inferiority or superiority complexes; both remained unknown to her. She was prompted simply by the natural instinct to protect those animals which formed a part of her life. At one time she lived with seventeen cats, who possessed the freedom to roam around her small house. Each one had a name, and she followed their relationships with interest. In the cat family Warda was Dodahi's daughter, and Haba' the old tom who spent most of the day asleep, was the fourth grandfather to Tameesa. He had reached the grand old age of fourteen and had in the process eaten seven of his offspring. Each of the seventeen had its own characteristics, and Auntie Asma never tired of repeating them to all who visited her.

XI

Like every schoolchild, our first day at the Fakhriya School was, in the broadest sense of the word, a day to remember. Only three other pupils from the previous school were similarly elevated to this school. Ahmad al-Haballo, who would become al-Duhul, Hasan Hammar,[18] and a third whose name I can't recall. The remaining pupils came largely from several other preparatory schools, most of which were private institutions. This private Fakhriya School was more like a collective institute and, in common with other schools, had a curriculum divided into three preparatory years, followed by an elementary section of three years, and lastly a senior section for a similar duration of time. The final year was called the *qubba*, and the graduates were regarded as equivalent to Ph.D. graduates today! Many of them went on to become teachers in that same school or in the Holy Mosque, while others became clerks or top civil servants in the judicial departments of the government.

Coming from a preparatory school, we were admitted into the first year of the elementary section together with twenty others, half of them from this school, the rest from others. Unlike today, when fourth year pupils range from nine to ten years old, our class comprised boys ranging in age from eleven to twenty. Appearances varied too; there was the stone mason's son who arrived on his first day carrying a *showhat* that he stood up behind the door, or at the other extreme a civil servant's son who came wearing a Turkish fez on his head. Ahmad al-Duhul, who was in a class by himself, wore an *igal*, which was no more than a black rope wound around the head

27

to form a headband. Other boys wore turbans, some went bareheaded. Although none seemed unduly out of place, to this day I can recall with wonder the incongruous mixture of dress, ages, nicknames, and social standing that were distributed among us.

Although tolerance was the general rule, a quarrel broke out on the first day between Hasan Hammar and a rich man's son. The latter insulted the former by making disparaging remarks about his father. It seems that Hasan was not unprepared for possible jibes, and answered his antagonist by saying that a person need not be embarrassed by his status in life, only by wrong actions, and that *Sayyiduna* Ali was a porter, and so and so was a camel-driver, etc. While this succeeded in reluctantly silencing his accuser, the latter waylaid Hasan after school and tried once again to provoke a fight to decide the winner in the morning's dispute.

Our first subject of the day was grammar. The teacher so arranged the class that the pupils sat in rows on the floor, the tallest and oldest at the back and the shortest at the front. He then conducted a brief review to ascertain how much we knew already, and how much we'd forgotten. The overall response to his questions was a negative one, an apathy in part induced by the long summer holiday, and to which the teacher was accustomed. Accordingly, he moved on from the general to the specific, asking particular questions about parsing, types of verbs, and weak verbs. He directed his first question at Ahmad, asking the latter to parse a sentence from the Quran. Ahmad, with his usual precocity, said, "This is too easy, Sir," and then proceeded to give a ludicrous answer. Then in return, the master called him "al-Duhul." Ahmad, from that day on became known as Ahmad al-Duhul ("the simpleton"). While unable to formulate the right answer, we others were too discreet to risk earning a name for stupidity. Having ascertained that we had remembered almost nothing of our previous year's grammar, he took it upon himself to remedy our deficiency. He began by dividing words into nouns, verbs and particles, the verbs into past, imperfect and imperative, and nouns into weak and sound, and with such facility that no one could follow him. And when the first period was over, he informed us that having summarily reviewed last year's curriculum, we would now embark on the new one. He went out, leaving the class in a state of stunned confusion which persisted until one of the older pupils, or "giants" as we called them, spoke for all of us when he said: "What's the matter with him? He talks like a machine. Did anyone understand anything?"

Rightly or wrongly, the sciences were not incorporated into our curriculum. Either they were considered heretical or the school was unaware of
their existence. Our learning was orthodox and in no way infractioned the
law; it might be said that our classes pivoted around the construing of what
the religious law permitted. When we were given a geography book with
a map of the Arab world at the front, Ahmad al-Duhul remarked in
surprise: "What's this Sir? Isn't representation forbidden?"[19] *Shaikh* al-
Shangeeti[20] who was conducting the period, opined that representation
was of two sorts, the forbidden and the permitted, and that drawing maps
was of the second kind.

In the years to come, and with a deeper knowledge of what was
sanctioned, we learned that the practice of masturbation, common to all
young men as part of their sexual development, was not considered
permissible unless it happened spontaneously, by the friction caused in
riding a camel, for example, or by some other such effect.

XII

Relations between the "giants" and the younger boys were most often
contentious. The latter were frequently beaten up, their books and pencils
stolen, their clothes badly torn, and they were subjected to ridicule. Their
one protector was al-Duhul, who often got so mad that he would rain kicks
and blows upon the strong in defense of the weak, his huge body and
powerful muscles presenting a formidable opposition.

And, having caught one of the bullies, he would squeeze his nose until
the boy begged for mercy. He would even come to the aid of those young
or weak teachers who were similarly threatened by these toughs. There was
the incident of our late history teacher who did not know how to answer
one of the "giants" who threatened to waylay him in an alley. The only
thing he could say to him was: "Even if you are strong, God is stronger."
The alley where fights broke out regularly was called the Abu Righal Alley.
It was next to the school, and it was here that accounts were settled between
pupils. We none of us knew the origin of its name or whether it was in some
way associated with the infamous Abu Righal,[21] and, failing to attract the
attention of local historians, its history died out, just as the history of all
alleys and byways of Mecca have.

Uniformity of appearance applied no more to the teachers than to the pupils. The more dignified of the masters wore a cloak and a turban, with a shawl arranged over their turban. Others wore a gown and waistcoat, and a turban wound around the head by the wearer himself. Still another type favored a starched, peaked *taqiyya*. They varied in age from the very young to those who were endowed with the experience of sixty or seventy years of age. Their personalities were as individual as the manner of their speech. Our *Shaikh* al-Shangeeti, for instance, spoke classical Arabic, chanting his sentences, and vowelizing the last letters in a way that stressed his mastery of the Arabic language.[22] He spent much of his teaching time in attempting to correct our manner of speech, something which occasioned a sharp dispute between him and al-Duhul. The latter insisted on ignoring the *Shaikh*'s prescribed rules of grammar, and would insolently yell out, "We don't understand anything, *Shaikh*. Speak Arabic," meaning "Speak colloquial." But whatever the faults or inadequacies of the teaching methods of those days, we were made to cultivate the art of memory. We had to memorize most of our knowledge in verse form from *al-Alfiyya* of Ibn Malik[23] in grammar, to al-Rahbiyya in the science of religious precepts and Islamic law of descent and distribution; and even parts of our geography texts were versified:

Africa is bounded on the left side
By Tunis, O expert in affairs worldwide.

Our professors must also be credited for the wide horizons of their knowledge. They taught Islamic jurisprudence not from one source, but from several orthodox schools. Thus, each group was permitted to study their fathers' faith, be it Hanafi, Shafi'i, Maliki, or whatever,[24] and, accordingly our books were full of valuable hypotheses that took into account changes of law that might occur in the future. Discussions were wide-ranging, and I recall our dispute over the legality of eating fish from a river if a river should flow through Mecca, most of the teachers being disposed to view such a practice as unlawful, while the students held the view that it was a permissible action. And as for the students who were Meccans, and therefore better informed about Mecca's valleys, etc., they saw the dispute as an opportunity to poke fun at those teachers who were not originally from Mecca.

Other topics also came up for discussion. The elements which violated the ritual of ablution before prayer were the subject of extensive elucidation from the teacher of Maliki jurisprudence. By raising a particular question, he demonstrated how narrow were the confines of our thinking. With an explicitness that surprised us, he asked, "If what is ejected from the two body exits violates ritual purity, will handling one of them also violate it? That is, if one carries a vessel containing impurities, what is the proper judgement?"

When Ahmad suggested he refrain from touching on such coarse subjects, he replied: "There's nothing shameful in religion."

XIII

We often hear mentioned that a certain event or chance encounter was responsible for radically transforming a person's way of life and thinking. I suppose I could say this of the six years I spent at that school before graduating with the highest certificate attainable the length and breadth of the country. Like any major transformation, it began gradually, then built up its own momentum to the exploding point with a subsequent calm. Such, anyhow, was the case with Muhaisin al-Baliy, the author's fictional surrogate in this book.

It took time to adjust to the new school and surroundings, but eventually I was able to formulate a clear perspective of my environment. One teacher proved insufferable, while another was good-hearted almost to the point of naiveté. But that did not matter, for one of the greatest narrators of the Prophet's traditions in olden times was, may God bless him, of a gullible nature. We liked this place in the classroom more if our teacher was the history teacher, and we liked the other more if he was the Arabic language teacher. I liked my Arabic language class and hated my history class.

I developed a preference for al-Duhul's company on the way home from school, and our route took in Hameedeeya Street rather than Barseem Alley. Our decision to take this street was motivated by the fact that we usually encountered a friend there with his pockets full of *nabaq*, or lotus fruit, or sometimes with flat, round millet loaves, which he would share with us out of courtesy. If I had lunch at Bab al-'Umra, it meant that I could save part of the piaster which was my spending money for the day. Thus I came to establish a complete program for the events of the day, both in school and out. This took all the first part of the school year.

In the second year we began studying a book called *Al-Alfiyya of Ibn Malik*. Although the book of *Al-Alfiyya* is known only to a few, it is well worth studying, and greatly contributes to one's knowledge of the Arabic language. You would then acquire the knowledge of our Shangeeti *Shaikh*, may God rest his soul, although you wouldn't find it necessary to adopt his manner of chanting.

Right from the start, *Al-Alfiyya* was a book that posed considerable problems for our class. We had again and again to ask the *shaikh* to elucidate almost every word in each paragraph under study, until God, as we hoped, would assist our understanding. If one of us intimated that he had understood a passage, the *shaikh* would proceed to the second verse of *al-Alfiyya*, resigning himself to the probability that the rest had failed to comprehend and despairingly summing up his frustration by saying aloud, "What is it to me if the camels don't understand?"

Many of the more backward students not only flunked their examinations at the end of the year, but dropped out of school permanently. Hasan Hammar was one of these. He protested that this sort of learning was of little value to his future and that he would rather seek out a profitable trade. As for myself, I found the unraveling of *al-Alfiyya*, Ibn Malik's abracadabra, a positive challenge that I was determined to pursue. I began to assimilate its meaning during the third year, a period of my life that I shall come to refer to as the year of funerals. It was during that third year that one day our teacher entered the room at noon, studying a particularly abstruse verse. As usual he asked for someone to volunteer to explain the meaning of this verse, assured that the response would be negative. He had no sooner begun interpreting the work himself, than he was taken aback by my slowly raising my finger in request to explain the designated piece. I could see that he was speechless with surprise, and dumbfounded that a pupil should show willingness to venture a commentary on this verse. To everyone's surprise I succeeded with my explanation, despite the sweat that trickled down my spine, and my terrible selfconsciousness. I had prepared myself mentally for the occasion, and the enthusiasm generated by my success had the *shaikh* announce that "God has a way of bestowing his blessings, even to the ant." I didn't realize at the time that his remark constituted disparagement in the form of praise, and thereafter, as a consequence of my initiative, I was morally obliged to daily prepare the groundwork for the class in the rules of grammar. In time I grew to assist the *shaikh* by expounding the verses to the class preparatory to his own advanced commentary, thus allowing him to relax, or perhaps to doze off a little while I spoke. In fact, I acted as a teacher's assistant, giving the preliminaries of the lesson, prior to the *shaikh's* intervention. I discovered that, like anything else in life, one could accustom oneself to the al-Alfiyya and consequently comprehend its style. I became so taken up with the study of the latter that I was constantly on the lookout for double meanings, for which I would ask an explanation. The teacher would invariably choose one of the two explanations, while I, partly to expose his ignorance, chose the harder of the two meanings. Having exposed my pedantic fastidiousness with grammatical science, I was asked to attend his class in the Holy Mosque near the *Umm* Hani Gate every afternoon. I did so, hesitatingly at first because of the age difference between myself and the students there and the difficulty I encountered in following al-Ashmuni's supercommentary on Ibn Aqeel's commentary on Ibn Malik's *al-Alfiyya*. However, the instinct to survive fortified me in a lesson that remained incomprehensibly difficult.

XIV

I have had occasion already to refer to my third year as one characterized by funerals. After the proceedings of my uncle's funeral, I had not had the occasion to pray over the dead, until I joined the classes of the Holy Mosque. No day passed there without prayer over a dead man or woman, perhaps sometimes more than one, and once the prayer was said in absentia. I learned too to differentiate between the burial of a man and a woman, the latter always having an elevated arch placed on her chest as a distinguishing sign. Likewise, I learned to distinguish those who were descendants of the Prophet[25] through the green sash wrapped around their biers, and that there was a distinction between funerals of the rich and poor, the latter occasions being ill-attended and accorded little ceremony.

I came to know the procedure intimately — the prayers delivered for the dead, the funeral procession, which went by way of the Salam Gate to the Mudda'a, then to its final stage — the graveyard. My association with this ritual grew until I found myself following every deceased person to his final resting place, engaging in the service due one Muslim by another: "And if one of you dies, follow him."[26] The graveyards at this time were without the protection of walls, so that packs of dogs marauded in that territory, and were partly responsible for the remains of the dead which were often to be found exposed above ground. I discovered that there were elitist burial grounds and common ones, as well as a spot near the gate serving those whose families did not specify any special burial ground. Through trial and error I learned to distinguish one funeral from another by the number of mourners in evidence. By the clothes they wore I could anticipate at first sight whether we were to bury a distinguished person or an obscure one who would be consigned to the gate. A poor man's bier might have as few as four people in attendance. As a strange mental exercise, I became obsessed with searching the faces of the living to determine how they would end. Those with elegant, starched clothes I called the elite, anticipating that they would be buried after a comfortable life in a place prepared for the notables of society.

I became engrossed by funerals. No corpse was prayed over but I followed it, and may God forgive me if I say that some of the dead resembled the living. Some were likable and some were not, but no matter my feelings, I never failed to help throw earth on a dead person's grave or to watch him being lowered into it. And in the course of so doing I memorized the entire *sura* of Ya Sin[27] — our burial recital. "So glory be to Him, whose hand holds dominion over all things, and unto Him you shall be returned."[28]

Unpredictable things happen to the dead just as they do to the living. It may be that a grave allocated to one of the deceased is found unsuitable for that purpose, due sometimes to the fact that the bones of the dead person who preceded him had not yet sufficiently decayed to permit another interment. This being the case, the grave is closed, and the sexton digs another. "No soul knows in what land it will die."[29] The sight of putrefying matter, of faces from which life had departed, of bones and hair and remains that I often stumbled upon, and the stench that arose from graves that had partly collapsed, all helped to create in me a marginal attachment to life. My gravitation in that third year at school was toward death. I eventually withdrew from contact with the living; after having performed my duty toward the dead for several months, I stopped helping to bear the coffins, as this involved contact with people, either those who assisted at the funeral, or the mourners to whom one had to offer condolences. I had arrived at a psychological condition which could be termed a state of continual nausea. The latter involved both mental and physical symptoms, so that the malaise became a psychophysical neurosis that had the effect of poisoning me. My mother even came to think that I had been jinxed by malefactors who begrudged me my success in life and had given me something harmful to eat or drink. My mother was confirmed further in her beliefs by the nature of the dreams I underwent during this period of my life. They all revolved around the image of a savage beast which was about to devour me. I would scream in my sleep, then wake up shaking and in a cold sweat from the tenor of the dream. The odd thing about the dream imagery was that the threatening beast either originated or ended in the shape of a huge dung beetle. My treatment necessitated repeated visits to pious people, together with drinking vast quantities of *mahw*, water in which charms written in China ink had been soaked. If I were a psychoanalyst, visited by someone whose life I was familiar with in every circumstance, my analysis would read as follows: "A whole series of circumstances have contributed to this young man's condition. Firstly, his having arrived at maturity this year, when, as the common folk say, the sap of manhood flows in the limbs. The latter phenomenon has brought about many organic and psychological changes, in addition to an increase in bodily height. And this combined with poor nourishment and a morbid preoccupation with the dead and the sight of decaying corpses, accounts for his nervous state. Those savage beasts are nothing but the dung beetles and scorpions seen in the bottom of graves. Stored up by the subconscious, they take on monstrously inflated proportions when released by the mind in sleep."

Yes, if I were a psychoanalyst presented with this case, my reasoning would run along those lines. But my problem is that I, Muhaisin al-Baliy, am not a psychoanalyst, and I still lack an explanation for what came over me at the time. I felt like someone who was semi-paralyzed, not in an arm or leg, where paralysis most commonly strikes, but in the brain. I lived in a sort of trance and collided with people in the street and with pillars in the Holy Mosque when roaming around aimlessly in the porticos.

Despite the fragility of my life, I persisted in my study of al-Ashmuni's supercommentary. If anything, I became more absorbed in it than before, almost it seemed in an effort to utilize every cell in the unparalyzed hemisphere of my brain in that circle at Umm Hani Gate. What I gained from this devotion to study was the enrichment of knowing by heart a vast corpus of strange and unique poetry, which referred to the views of one or the other noted grammarian. At the time I became a fervent advocate of the Basra School of Arabic grammar in contradistinction to the Kufa School.[30]

And through this I discovered that a person may adopt a prejudice in relation to a place they have never seen. To this day I prefer Basra to Kufa, although I am unfamiliar with both, and despite the possibility that Kufa may have become a much more attractive city than Basra.

By the end of that year my obsession with funerals declined and my passion was concentrated mostly on the study circles at the Holy Mosque. The most remarkable of these circles were those in which Arabic language lessons were given in some of the languages of East Asia, just as it was customary for the Ottomans to give us Arabic grammar in Turkish.

My phase of nausea also ended about this time, and it seemed appropriate to call this psychological development, after such a bad year, my spring equinox. It was my radical improvement which compelled my mother to fulfill her vow. She bought a lamb, stewed it in the manner of the renowned dish of the time, cooked with an agreeable mixture of rice and chickpeas, and fed it to the poor.

Whether it was a psychological state of nausea, a possession that had to be exorcised, or simply the difficult demands of puberty, however one comes to interpret it, the graveyards ceased to be of interest to me. But, of course, prayer for the dead continued for the duration of my association with the porticos of the Mosque and its recesses.

XV

I no longer had occasion to see Sufyan except if we happened to meet by chance in the narrow street running between al-Sululi Square and Ajyad Gate. When two people meet there, they cannot avoid each other, so they either exchange greetings or avert their heads as an act of dismissal. Thus, it is one of the few streets in the world where one is compelled to manifest one's feelings towards the person encountered. Meeting there, I could not possibly turn my face away from my boyhood companion, despite some of the painful experiences he had inflicted on me. The encounter only lasted a few minutes, long enough for me to inquire about the circumstances of his life and for him to ask about certain of our old friends. After which we went our separate ways.

Quite unexpectedly, Sufyan knocked on our door one Friday mid-morning, reminding me of that portentous Friday in the past. Asking God to protect me from temptation, I decided in myself not to be lured out with

36

him, for, despite the numerous references in classical poetry to "the beheading of men," I was not going to risk a repeat performance of viewing an execution. However, accepting his assurance that nothing of the sort would happen this time and curious to know of his intentions, I put myself in God's hands and left with him.

This time Sufyan pursued a new direction, and we entered a narrow alley not far from our house, called Jabart[31] Alley because of the presence of a *rabat* carrying the same name.

After having covered the area beyond this alley, we started climbing toward the old mountain called The Seven Girls. We had completed half of our climb when two security police came into view, positioned in front of one of those small houses couched on the slopes of the various mountains of Mecca. Involuntarily, I froze in my tracks and then instinctively started moving backwards, but Sufyan, who stood firm, stopped me with one stern look. I resumed walking at his heels, following the arc he described to the right of the two security police. We traveled in a circle, and, by making a detour which I did not understand at first, he led me to an area on the blind side of the guards and wide of the house. Then, without any explanation, he climbed up the branch of a thorn tree close to the house and entered through an upper window. I had no other choice but to follow him, although my legs were shaking involuntarily, threatening to make me fall from that lofty height.

We entered the room and found nothing to attract our immediate attention. It was a room like any other, containing a simple Shirazi rug, some cushions and mattresses, and little else. Sufyan quickly crossed this room to another on the right where it appeared something had definitely taken place. Everything in the room was upside down: the vessels, cups and mattresses. Congealed blood stains spattered the furnishings. Unsure of what to make of this, I began questioning Sufyan by motioning to him with my hands, but he silenced me by placing his index finger to his lips. Then, retracing our steps through the first room, we climbed out of the window, down the thorn tree, and proceeded back down the mountain. When we had almost reached my home, Sufyan launched into an explanation. "The blood we saw," he said, "was that of *Amm* Bakhtyar's. He was killed last night by Ali al-Iskharbuti, the seller of *sobya* whose shop stands near the al-Safa Gate. He killed him because he caught him with his sister, whom he also killed, before giving himself up at the police station with his knife in his hand. Those two policemen are guarding the house until the evidence

is assembled for a court-case. The two bodies were removed before dawn."
He went on to say that Muhammad Ali would be killed the coming Friday
as an act of punishment. But the latter prediction was wishful thinking,
and the event still has not occurred almost three quarters of a century later.

I was left with a sense of disappointment, largely I expect due to my
inner self secretly demanding an event more thrilling than that which
Sufyan had shown me. Somehow the sight of the blood stains didn't seem
worth the trip.

While the event made no immediate impression on me, I imagine now,
when it springs to mind, that it may affect my offspring in generations to
come, and may perhaps show up at a much later date. According to what
I have been told, everything one sees or hears, whatever happens to one, or
whatever one chances upon is stored up in the subconscious mind before
manifesting itself in the form of an ancestral dream, or in patterning one's
daytime behavior if it has had a powerful effect on the cells and genes.
Consequently, I don't see why it should be thought improbable that a
person, male or female, a thousand years from now, should have a vision
during sleep in which he imagines he is bathing in a sea of dried blood with
a person resembling Sufyan, who has sprouted a horn on his forehead and
stands beside him emitting loud peals of devilish laughter. It's not
impossible that a grandson or granddaughter might baffle a psychoanalyst
with such a vision. The latter would be hard put to account for the quantity
of blood, in the same way that our contemporaries today find themselves
unable to rationalize the phenomena that occur in our generation.

If it weren't for my just having read the informative report published by
the International Life Organization about murders, suicides, and the like,
my memory would not have taken me back to al-Iskharbuti and others.
That momentous report, consisting of over five hundred pages, comprises
a world survey of human societies: some agricultural, others industrial,
dark-eyed or blue-eyed according to race, living either in a warm climate
with winter rainfall, or in a climate characterized by temperate summers,
etc. After investigating the various kinds of crimes in circulation, modern
ways of committing suicide, and the organizations that advise the suicidal
on the most effective means of self-disposal, the report goes on to state that
the highest rate of crime and suicide occurs in the northern industrialized
societies.

While I don't take exception to this invaluable report, I do wish it would
conclude with a sentence reading thus: "The industrialized and non-

industrialized societies," for reasons I shall explain. Along with the aforementioned al-Iskharbuti incident, I heard during that time of the fatal occurrence in which al-Malakni's daughter burned herself by dousing her hair with kerosene and setting fire to it. And at least two people threw themselves into the bathhouse well at the foot of Mount Khandama. A third body was raised from another well with which I'm not acquainted. In addition, someone I knew died after drinking a lethal substance.

As far as I know, none of these people were blue-eyed, nor do I recall that we were living in the north in those days.

With the inclusion of this simple postscript I have proposed, the report could be considered accurate to the highest degree.

XVI

One day after the lesson in the Holy Mosque, our late and dearly missed professor suddenly surprised me by introducing a topic I had not anticipated. He told me confidentially that he was planning to hold a private class in his house for a small group after the evening prayer. He would take advantage of this opportunity to read with them a new book on a subject other than grammar. Having recognized my thirst for knowledge, he had singled me out to be one of the privileged. After describing his house in the Misfala quarter, he said he hoped I would attend punctually, so as not to miss any of his instruction.

To realize that one had been selected from a large group of people to become a special student was matter enough to induce feelings of self-satisfied importance. However, Mother resolutely rejected the idea. She discouraged me from going to any house other than our own, Auntie Asma's, or those of our immediate neighbors. In those days it was considered a late hour for a child of my age to be out after evening prayer, a tradition maintained by those of our generation who were accustomed to the nighttime being for the family and daytime for the outside world. But that night, when Mother refused my request, I showed disobedience toward her. Refusing to eat the supper she set before me or to go to bed at the appointed time, I sat up long after she had extinguished the house-lantern and stared into the darkness. In the middle of the night she came to me, and tried to persuade me of her point of view, but I remained adamant. It wasn't so much a desire for learning that motivated my persistence, for how can someone covet the acquisition of a subject yet unknown to him, but the feeling of shame I felt, and the sense of embarrassment I would undergo on facing the teacher with the excuse of my mother's refusal to allow me to go to his house with the other chosen students. It was these factors which determined my insistence on joining the circle. Her refusal did not last long. Before midnight she conceded, leaving the matter in God's hands, as she expressed it, earnestly praying that no harm would come to me in my newly chosen course. She advised me to walk in the middle of the street, and not on the side, as we do today, to use the main thoroughfares, to avoid the dark alleys, to keep myself constantly alert to the possibilities of danger, and above all to follow her instructions in every detail.

The first night he, may God bless his memory, distributed to us copies of a book called *al-Milal wa al-Nihal*,[32] by an author I didn't know. Unable to comprehend the meaning of the two words that comprised the title, I stared at them fixedly, as though by that act of concentration I would be provided with the means to unravel the riddle which eluded me. That proving unfeasible, I resorted to silence, that great virtue which has so often come to the aid of mankind when faced with an insoluble conundrum.

Our group was few in number — seven to be exact — none of whom I had met before that night, and I did not ask who they were. In those days people did not really introduce themselves as they do today on encountering a stranger, nor did they ask about his name or identity. Visiting cards were unknown, and our teacher expressed no interest in having his group become better acquainted. Each of us remained isolated in the small circle we formed in readiness for the lesson. There is a symbolism attached to the circle that has not yet been fully explored, for, as I remember, we sat around the dining room table in a circle, our classes in the mosque described a circle, and our circumambulation of the Kaaba was a circular movement. And the tradesmen in the vegetable market at that time also formed a circle. Even the minds of our contemporary poets soared in the heights of poetry, that is they whirled around in a complete or a vicious circle.

We did not have to wait long to begin. The *shaikh* started with an introduction to the author: his birth, his early life, the derivation of his name, and the location of the village to which his ancestry could be traced.

40

This allowed us to feel on familiar terms with the author, as if close ties had existed between us previously, or at least a sympathetic relationship.

Likewise, the title of the book—and a book is known by its title—became clear to us by the end of the lesson, a period that claimed my undivided attention. When the class came to an end, the books were gathered and placed in a pile at the side of the room.

As I remember it, nothing out of the ordinary occurred until a young skinny boy, probably a servant, offered us small glasses of a red liquid unfamiliar to me. Remembering my mother's advice, I looked suspiciously at the contents of the glasses. I could tell it wasn't the customary tea; the color wasn't one I associated with tea, and the coolness of the glass contradicted the heat of tea. I hesitated to sip it and instead waited for the others to begin. When their features showed no evidence of displeasure at the taste, I ventured to try a sip. The experience was displeasing, so I stopped and stared up at the ceiling, hoping by that action to avoid the teacher's eyes. Noticing my reluctance to drink, he said: "Drink Muhaisin, this licorice root is good for the nerves and blood." He elaborated no further. The name was at once strange to me in addition to its being unpleasant to the ears. I resolved to give it one or two more tries, faking enthusiasm for something I did not relish. Thereafter, I concentrated on trying to find a spot in the room where I could dispose of the contents of my glass, pretending it was an accident but at the same time studiously avoiding the household furnishings. My equivocation was short-lived; it seems I was under observation. Deciding to rescue me from my predicament, the *shaikh* took the glass and gave it to the servant, saying: "The taste of this drink does not please Muhaisin." I took a deep breath, as I did not know then how to heave a deep sigh.

Undoubtedly, my suspicion was generated not so much by the taste of licorice, but the fear I had grown up with concerning everything new or strange, in part resulting from my mother's daily refrain: "Take care you don't drink anything from the hand of a stranger. Don't eat in other people's houses. Don't go in. Don't come out. Don't."

My own experience of the encounter with licorice root was not unlike the situation of the Arabian journalist who traveled to Egypt, much later than my incident, and who refused to drink that which was offered him, saying, "I don't drink alcoholic beverages." When it was pointed out to him that the drink wasn't alcoholic, but something comparatively harmless called Coca Cola, he only added: "Changing the name doesn't change what it is. The name in itself doesn't sound pleasant." Embarrassed by the situation, his Egyptian host ordered a cup of coffee to pacify this Arab *shaikh* come from the desert.

The lessons proceeded well if that means they followed one another, subject to the dictates of a schedule; but if one is to take into account enthusiasm for the subject presented and easy assimilation of it, then things didn't progress as well as I and other members of the group would have wished. Our progress was slow. Moving from one page to the next seemed more difficult than making an Atlantic crossing.

After attending for a number of evenings, I came to the conclusion that the subject should be handled differently, so I stayed on at the end of the lesson in order to be alone with the *shaikh*. I asked him bashfully if it would be possible for me to borrow his copy of *Al-Milal wa al-Nihal*, in order to prepare the lessons beforehand. He agreed on condition that I take good care of the book lest the covers or pages be soiled or torn. This improved the situation, and made it easier for me to follow what was going on in class. As a consequence I even ventured to ask questions and join in the debate established by conflicting religious groups. Despite all that, I never managed to complete the journey to the end. I do not know which straw, that is which religious community, broke the camel's back — my back. It may have been the Rafidites sect or the Jahmiyya sect,[33] or both of them. The main result was that I slowed my pace, rather as people do in today's organized strikes. The employees slow down on entering the factory and maintain that dilatory momentum all day long, thereby lowering their output and consequently affecting the economy of the enterprise. This then draws attention to their requests. In this way they don't manifest civil disobedience, and so are not punishable by law; but, unsatisfied with their lot, they would not forfeit the chance to better their situation. The first time I arrived a few minutes late, the group waited for me, and they acted likewise on the second occasion, although the *shaikh*'s loud clearing of his throat when he heard me crossing the passage leading from the outer door of the room warned me that his patience had limits. The third time I delayed until the lesson was over, then returned home having loitered aimlessly in the alleys. The incident afforded me my first experience of that curious sensation known as bilocation, when someone thinks you are in one place when in fact you are in another. As a consequence you smile to yourself as though you were hiding the biggest secret of the age. Later, I returned the book to the *shaikh* saying: "Due to special circumstances, I am unable to continue in the class." He did not ask about my reasons, and I did not properly understand them myself. All I know is that the deluge of intellectual chaos enclosed within the covers of that book did not appeal to me. I mean it did not captivate me sufficiently to merit finishing the course. Every argument used to support a certain school or sect seemed to me logical until the *shaikh* began refuting them one after the other, with his usual practice of beginning with: "The answer to that, if you are asked, is..." Proceeding until he had exhausted the topic, he would move on to another. In the end I failed to understand the necessity of substantiating arguments in order to disprove them so easily.

If I derived any benefit from the time I devoted to this study, it was that it instilled in me the capacity to enter into a debate on any subject that captured my enthusiasm, and to present the other side of my point of view so proficiently that I once considered, many years later, pursuing the profession of law or becoming an advocate, as the present generation terms it. I felt I was capable of defending any case that carried my conviction. However, as I knew that people most often get punished by the words they utter, I preferred to retain my well-being, rather than become the sort of lawyer who faces ruin as a consequence of his speech.

XVII

Our numbers diminished considerably in the high school, leaving only a small group, of which I was one. My chief regret was that we lost al-Duhul, whose shadow alone was sufficient to strike fear into those who bullied the small, weak boys. There was a young man in our group at the time called Husam al-Askar. Although right from the start neither of us took to each other, we were both so occupied with our own respective affairs that we did not clash despite our never having so much as exchanged greetings. It is possible that he may have been an ancestral enemy and his image become translated into my psyche, thus accounting for my initial antipathy to him. Or I may have represented a relative he hated, thereby making us incompatible through the influence of an intermediary. But now, with al-Duhul's departure, he was presented with the opportunity to begin provoking me. Seeing that I was the smallest student in the class, it appeared certain that any combatant's challenge would undoubtedly have me defeated and, in fact, I was defeated. My actual defeat only encouraged him to worsen his behavior. I, in turn, adopted the strategy of avoiding al-Askar, not with the intention of neutralizing his feelings, but more to keep him at a distance. My first tactic was to escape as soon as the last class was over, and I did this by carrying my sandals under my arm, tucking up my gown, for fear I trip on it, and then running as fast as I could toward the boundaries of our quarter where I would be seen by the shopkeepers in that area. My method proved successful until al-Askar fathomed my strategy. He started leaving ahead of me, and, cutting off my route of escape, he would provoke me into a skirmish. Eventually this became part of my daily routine. No matter how I developed ways to defend myself, ways which included biting and trying to grab him in the genitals, I would invariably prove the loser. In addition, my defense tactics were considered unmanly by the fighting conventions of the day. It became a preoccupation with me to think of ways to avoid his brutality, and one evening I stumbled on a solution.

I was returning from the mosque shortly after the evening prayer, and, on reaching the entrance to our house, I sensed that a person, or the outline of an indistinct shape, was standing there with what appeared to be a large bag or a sack on his back, an item perhaps larger than the body of the one carrying it. I opened the door quickly and got inside, leaving no occasion for that menacing shape to speak to me. No sooner had I gotten inside than someone began knocking and calling to me in a whisper: "Muhaisin, Muhaisin." The knocker was Sufyan. On realizing that, the hair on my head stood up with fright as I imagined him to be carrying a dead body or a murdered person on his back. But his persistent knocking and whispering left me no other course than to open the door a crack, enabling me to hear him say: "Let me leave this bag in your vestibule for a few days." My response was unhesitatingly inspired, and I found myself saying: "On the condition that we fight al-Askar." I had not thought for a moment of what might be in the sack, nor of the possible consequences arising from concealing it in our house. I could only think about defeating al-Askar. With no hesitation Sufyan replied: "Agreed. But who is this al-Askar whom you want me to fight?" "Husam," I said. "Who is Husam?" he asked. "A fellow student," I said. "Nothing to it," was his response. I opened the

44

door to him and he carried his load to that spot at the end of the vestibule where it was necessary to bend over if one wanted to reach the alcove in which we stored our charcoal. There, dumping his load on the floor, he maneuvered it into the south corner where it couldn't be observed either by those entering or leaving. When he returned to the door, I stopped him with a wave of my hand. "And al-Askar?" I said. "I'll wait for you tomorrow afternoon when you come out of school," he replied. "All you have to do when you see me is to point him out, and I'll do the necessary."

The next day I was a witness to how revenge can pacify the frightened heart, although my initial reaction was not a feeling of peace and serenity but a strong heaving of my chest as I watched, terrified at what happened. For no sooner had I pointed out al-Askar's lamentable figure, with the slightest of gestures on emerging from school, than Sufyan approached him, and, without saying a word, gave him such a slap in the face that I understood in that instant the meaning of a blow rocking a person. It rocked him like an earthquake. He had probably never felt anything like this in his whole life. Before he lost his balance, Sufyan lifted him over his head and threw him to the ground. Then, kneeling on his chest, he first of all punched and kicked him before twisting his neck and rubbing his forehead in the dust. Then, taking the collar of his gown in his hands, he tore it in two, changing it into the semblance of a cloak worn at the time. Finally, he turned to me and asked, "Enough?" At the nod of my sanctioning head he left him where he was and, after pressing my hand, went on his way.

After that incident Husam was absent for a number of days. He returned wearing a new gown, his head closely cropped, and manifested a meek, submissive spirit that endured until we had both finished school and gone our separate ways. I had learned from this how weak creatures could exploit those superior in strength, if they only knew how to put to good use a chance incident arising from a dark vestibule.

That evening I was resolved to find out the contents of the sack that Sufyan had deposited in our charcoal alcove. I opened it with considerable trepidation, only to find that all it contained was an assortment of worn-out sandals. The latter discovery only served to increase my curiosity about the matter. A few days later I was to learn of what had happened.

A cobbler who stitched old sandals with the aid of an awl used to work by the fountain used for ritual ablution at Ajyad Gate. Sufyan felt like stealing them and, while the shoemaker had gone to the evening prayer, took the sack he sat on. After stuffing it with that great heap of sandals, he put it on his back and took off.

That same evening I sensed that Sufyan was going to come to the tragic end prophesied for him by *Shaikh* Ishaq: that one day he would be crucified and the birds would eat his head.

What he did with those old sandals was to sell them gradually. Taking two or three pair with him, he would go to one of the various cobblers and collect the going price, a few paltry *halalas* or piastres at best, until they were all gone. He confided in me that his best customer was a cobbler in Raquba Alley in the Mudda'a Quarter.

XVIII

One of the privileges of being in the upper school was that we were allowed to borrow books from the school library, something that we had shown no initiative in doing until several of the teachers encouraged us in a practice which was in keeping with the school tradition. I entered the principal's room to find him reclining against a cushion with a cup of tea and a straw flyswatter in front of him, with which he was whisking away flies. No sooner were the flies scattered than they regrouped and swarmed around the tea cup. The administrator would resume chasing them away, taking a sip of tea between each new raid. As soon as he saw me, he motioned me away without even bothering to inquire as to who I was or ascertain the purpose of my visit. However, contrary to his wishes, I did not leave, but walked up to him and said: "I'm Muhaisin." His reaction was to turn to the right and left as if wanting people to bear witness to an unaccustomed act. "Muhaisin?" he replied. "Who is this Musaisin?" "Muhaisin al-Baliy," I informed him, "a student in the upper section." "Ah! You want to borrow a book." Upon my replying in the affirmative, he reached towards a stack of books piled on a tattered cushion, pulled out the one his eye alighted on, and handed it to me, saying: "Take care, don't tear the pages, or put food on it and soil it." Having said that, he returned to his flies and tea, and I to my classroom. As I was to learn, that particular administrator owed his appointment to an Asian group that supported the school, and had been posted here for this assignment. He had taken over the administration of the library and the management and affairs of the school with the same manner of nonchalance with which he had dealt with me that morning. What could we do?

The book was a slim volume of poetry. It comprised a single *qaseeda* called *qaseeda* "Satirizing Time" by Abu So and So, the Andalusian. And I, with little knowledge of poetry, knew nothing about the subject except that we had studied it in our memorization classes, most notably the famous *qaseeda* of *al-Sumawa'al*[34]. I had extreme difficulty in understanding the verses and purpose of *qaseeda* "Satirizing Time." After reading it and consulting numerous teachers about the meaning of specific words and sentences, I ended up feeling sorry for Time that the author so disparaged. A number of the poem's verses remained with me for a considerable time afterwards, despite my having become absorbed in several other books, all of them consisting of defamatory poems. It was only later that I learned that the administrator persisted in giving these texts out in the same sequence to every borrower of school books. He may have been motivated by a shade of sadism, or, as a realist wished to show his pupils the dark side of life so that in the event that the other side shone through, their joy at that radiance would be twofold. I thank God that those particular books, together with al-Mutanabbi's famous satire on Dabba,[35] were the only satirical books advocated by the school. If not, I should have spent my remaining years there reading of nothing but the defamation of people's honor and character, and of those traits of behavior which are punishable by law. During my last two years at school I read widely and on diverse subjects. My reading incorporated novels and tales in translation, collections of poems and various other books, one of which was on Aristotle, and proved meaningless to me, a second on astronomy, and a third on metallurgy. This was an incongruous collection of books, not one of which I chose for myself, as our reading was selected by the presiding *shaikh*. Our group of readers, I hasten to add, consisted of three people, if I include myself.

I either did my reading in the mosque, due to the abundant light it afforded, or in an alley nearby lit by a municipal lamp. I would stand beneath the lamp to read and pace back and forth whenever my leg muscles started to cramp. I must have proved an odd sight, making passersby stop and wonder at this character who spent his nights reading and reading at the head of the street while sensible people were at home. However, the situation remained, for the lamp at home was not bright enough to assist my continuous reading. One of those who singled me out was *Amm* Umar, who lived at the end of the alley. He stopped on numerous occasions; the first time he inquired if I was the son of a certain lady. When I answered that I was, he went on to ask me what I was reading. Upon hearing my answer, he shook his head and hurried on. Whenever he noticed that I was reading a new book, he would repeat his question before going on his way. He was possessed of a strange and unique personality. He was probably the only adult in the quarter who had ever read a book outside of the usual school curriculum, the only one to hold a government post, and possibly the only one who wore a *jubba*, and then a *mishlah* when he continued as a government employee under the Saudi regime. He was always the first to experiment — he was the first to buy a radio as soon as they were invented, the first to wear prescription glasses, the first to purchase a car when cars were eventually imported, and created a precedent in hiring a servant other than the functional servants of the Hijaz, etc., and was responsible for many other innovations that I witnessed with the passing of time and the deepening of our relationship.

After my habit of reading on the corner of the street had persisted for a few months, *Amm* Umar stopped one evening to inform me that he had a large collection of books and would be pleased to lend me any I wished. I had only to call at his house any afternoon to look them over and select the ones I wished to read. I thanked him politely for his intended generosity, and he returned home.

The next day, in passing, he greeted me from a distance without commenting on our conversation of the previous day. After repeating this behavior for a number of evenings, he finally stopped to ask if I had forgotten the invitation he had extended to me. He confirmed that the invitation still held good, but, if I preferred, he would bring a number of books to show me in the street.

Feeling ashamed of myself, I said: "No there's no need for that. The reason I haven't taken up your offer is that I have a book on hand I am reading. After I finish it and return the book to the school, I'll gladly visit you."

In need of her advice, I told Mother that evening about the invitation which had been extended to me. She remained silent, evidently reflecting on my behavior the night she refused to grant me permission to attend the special course, and I had to ask her again. While she admitted to not wishing to stand in the way of my visit, she expressed a certain disquiet over *Shaikh* Umar's being a *farmasoni*, a Freemason. She insisted that the whole quarter knew of his beliefs. He was a frequent visitor to Christian countries, could speak a language other than that of the Muslims, and read huge books of mysterious content. "But if you insist on going," she said, "I shall accompany you the first time. I know his mother, she is a good woman, although she is now so old that she may not be able to fully recognize people. Nevertheless, I shall visit her, while you borrow the books and we'll return together."

Shaikh Umar might have been a Freemason or worse, I reflected on entering his sitting room and catching sight of a large picture of a bearded man who might have been his father or grandfather! Photographs were at that time considered next to mortal sin, and you would not have been able to find a single photographer's studio in our quarter, nor in the whole of Mecca. No one would have dared hang a picture, any picture, in his house, let alone a large exposure like that. Where on earth could he have brought it from?

I kept staring at the picture without crossing the threshold. How could I? Didn't the angels abandon a place where pictures were hung to devils and demons? When *Shaikh* Umar noticed my hesitation, he approached and offered his hand by way of greeting. Since there was nothing inauspicious about that gesture, I took his hand in mine and he smiled and said: "This is a picture of my father taken many years ago on a visit to London." London!!? Mother's warning returned to me, and I decided to be very cautious.

I went away with three books, without having once sat in that demon inhabited room. He didn't appear to have noticed my hesitation, and, when the time came for me to go, he said: "Return each book to me once you have read it." By this he meant that I should return the books one at a time without waiting to finish them all. I did so.

To his credit, he never once tried to delay me on returning one of his books, and he never asked me to sit down. I would greet him, return the book, then leave. It was not until I returned the third book that he invited me to sit down, so that he could show me a number of other books to choose from. On that occasion I was obliged to partake of tea and engage in a few moments of conversation with him. I did so, ready to jump at a moment's notice, but he did nothing but project that smile to which in time I was to grow accustomed.

But my reaction to his smile remained ambivalent — sometimes I felt it was friendly and at other times I hated it; it often had the same meaning as the verse: "What can I do if the camels don't understand?"

That day he asked me my opinion of the books I had borrowed and requested that I summarize the one which was a novel in translation. Immensely pleased with my performance, his sarcastic smile vanished and was replaced by a sparkle in his eyes. Immediately afterwards he led me into an inner room containing things beyond my wildest conception. There were hundreds of leather-bound books arranged on wooden shelves, stacked one above the other in perfect symmetry. What a Freemason he was!

Pointing to one of the rows, he said: "These are collections of our classical poets, and these are the *Mahjar* poets."[36] Of course, I couldn't follow him, and he continued with his commentary: "These are philosophical books, and these are on mathematics, and those over there are translated novels. He conspicuously left out a large section of books he had not pointed to, and I let the matter go. I had never before seen such a large collection of books assembled in one place. Compared to this private collection, the school library seemed impoverished and small. There wasn't a single book in our house. Not knowing how to react, I hesitated, until he encouraged me by saying: "You can take any one of these books provided you return it once you are finished with it." As I remained frozen, he took down a book and handed it to me, saying "I recommend this one."

As my admiration for this Freemason increased, in spite of my praying God to save me from evil, I found myself spending more time with him in his study, drinking tea and talking about one book or another. And the strangest thing of all was that the large picture hanging on the wall no longer disturbed me. One day I ventured to ask him how it was permissible to hang a forbidden image in his house. Instead of answering my question directly he, in turn, asked me if I had ever thought of worshipping that picture. Then he said nothing more on the subject. That was his way of deflecting many of the questions with which I assailed him. He would never answer directly, but always replied with another question and one of his peculiarly enigmatic smiles.

From the beginning he had told me: "Don't call me *Shaikh* Umar but *Ustadh* Umar." Gradually I came to call him *Ustadh*, and such was my respect for him that for a long time he was the only person I called *Ustadh*.

I don't know how many books I borrowed from him over this period of time, but I didn't read all of them in their entirety. If one appealed to me after reading a few pages, I would continue; if not, I would return it and take another.

This never perturbed him. In fact, after learning my tastes, he would help me choose. During the times I visited him to borrow and return books, we held conversations in which I would acquaint him with some of the happenings at school and ask his opinion about many topics, especially those concerning what was considered lawful and unlawful and what was permitted and not permitted. His replies were terse and seldom expansive. I once questioned him about an issue raised in class, wanting to know where he stood on the matter. Instead of expressing his opinion, he said: "Arguing about most of these things only manifests contempt for the human mind." That was all, nothing more. I didn't understand what he meant, but, as he was reluctant to expand, I too kept silent.

During that period of my life and throughout the final year, I began scribbling words on paper. I didn't know whether they were poetry, prose, or stories. None of them pleased me, so I tore them all up and started writing down proverbs I composed in the manner of the familiar proverbs, until I had a considerable collection of them. However, I lacked the ability to imitate those proverbs whose meaning eluded me. Their nature was obscure, like the one which read: "A camel-rider separated from the caravan makes no progress, and exhausts his camel."

Of my own proverbs I remember several. "Your tongue is part of you, even if it is short," something I derived by way of imitating the famous proverb: "Your nose is part of you, even if it is broken." And the saying, "Neither here nor there," I transformed into "Neither in the book nor in the street," meaning a person who succeeds neither in school nor in life in general. I carried a wad of blank slips of paper in one pocket, while the other was stuffed with the proverbs I had written, in order to revise them constantly and imitate according to my fashion. In the manner of the great writers who were always prepared for inspiration to arrive, I would leave the mosquito net, under which I slept, to search out my papers and write by lamplight, even in the middle of the night. I was obsessed with this power, especially after I had managed to accumulate almost one hundred

51

of what I considered to be the choicest proverbs ever coined, and ones which accommodated all situations. What afforded me the greatest pleasure was that I kept them secret. I would swagger along, puffed up with pride, my pockets swollen with paper, saying to myself: "If only people knew!" The task of revising, trimming or adding to was performed at least once a day. When I was convinced that my marvelous literary works had developed to their optimum value, I gathered up my collection and took them to the *Ustadh*, dissimulating my conceit and vanity by adopting a show of humility and intended embarrassment at the offering. I expected him to read them that very minute, and in doing so, acclaim their importance. However, he laid them aside without comment. His response did not so much sadden me as surprise me. How, I wondered, could anyone put off the perusal of those literary gems. But he did just that.

The following day I visited him, as to do so had become part of my daily routine. He returned my papers without uttering a word. After waiting in apprehension for his comments, I felt compelled, when it came time for me to leave, to ask him his opinion of my work. Giving me a long look he replied: "There's nothing original in them. They are all imitations of known proverbs. Try to write something that stimulates you." That was the last thing I expected. After all of my devoted labor, working day and night, all he could find to say to me was: "There's nothing original in what you have written!" I was so stung with anger that I was almost tempted to say: "Just show me one proverb 'you' have composed, even if that too is an imitation." But I held my peace. The worst thing was that he didn't try to soften or lighten the matter. He remained resolute, inflexible, silent as a stone, while I stood there dripping with perspiration, cracking my fingers together, one after the other. Eventually I could take no more, so, picking up my papers, I left in a rush, making for the door. Even then he made no move to restrain me. How I hated him that day! I wished upon him every evil that can befall a man by way of recompense for how he had humiliated me. "No doubt this is the true character of a Freemason," I told myself. "I shouldn't have had anything to do with him in the first place. I should have listened to Mother's admonitions." I spent that entire evening painfully out of sorts, unable to confide in anyone. Mother knew nothing about literature, although she had a store of common proverbs. I am by nature a sound sleeper. Every time I lay my head on the pillow I find myself completing last night's dream, but that particular night found me sleepless. I spent the better part of the night conducting a mental argument with the

Ustadh. I was trying to resolve what I should say to him when we met. Then his face would appear to me with that enigmatic smile on its lips, and my defenses would capitulate. I would try to establish new ones and, at the same time, attempt to understand the reason for his hostility, seeing that I couldn't remember ever having hurt him in word or deed.

Of course it never occurred to me that he could be right. That was the last thought to cross my mind. All that I could conceive was that he was motivated by jealousy, and it was the latter emotion that led him to belittle my exceptional achievement. That idea served to pacify me somewhat, but it led to no abatement of the tension that continued to erode me.

Eventually, my feeling of bitterness decreased. I went back to my pockets, took out that treasure-hoard of proverbs that I had abandoned for some days past, and endeavored to rework them, revising, improving, and reassessing their content, as if nothing had happened.

Naturally, I stayed away from the Freemason's house, and no longer borrowed books. I returned the last book of his I had in my possession, through my mother, who seemed pleased at the rift which had occurred between the *Ustadh* and me. This pained me for a reason I couldn't comprehend at the time. I also had to find an alternative reading place to the lamp in the alley, for I knew he went by there every day. After giving it careful thought, I asked Mother if she would consider buying a larger lantern for the house so I could dispense with the alley and keep up my reading inside the walls of our house. She agreed.

XIX

In our quarter — just like any other quarter in the world — there was a group of idiots. In this respect our district didn't differ from the Reeperbahn quarter in Hamburg or the area of Montparnasse in Paris, except in the name we conferred on the weak-minded. In Paris they are commonly known as artists or bohemians, while we term them imbeciles or those touched by God. Otherwise their behavior is similar, and they share the same tattered clothes, made out of patches. In Paris, moreover, they frequently patch their new clothes with pieces of vari-colored old cloth to conform to the latest styles in fashion. Thus, my former prophecy, that wearing patches would one day become the mark of the age, was fulfilled.

Some of the disturbed in our quarter loved to draw, and, as they were little encouraged in this pursuit, they would draw on the walls of houses, taking advantage of the surplus of charcoal that existed at the time to have easy access to drawing material. Some of those pictures could be designated as modern existentialism, as the majority of them depicted human figures who did not even cover their bodies with the proverbial fig leaf. Others could be categorized as attempts at expressionism, as the derangement of the artists led them to exaggerate the anatomies of the creatures they drew. When their artistic works were finished, they would ask some schoolboy to write the name of one of their fellow idiots beneath the picture. Those mischievous rascals would often substitute other names, thereby creating a fight between the idiot—I mean the artist—and the one whose name appeared under it. The argument would usually end with the owner of the name insisting that his name be erased by the idiot, who, in turn, would insist that it wasn't the name of the complainant but of someone else, while at the same time taunting his adversary with the recrimination: "Don't you know how to read? Are you insane?"

The worst of these fights took place when an idiot renowned for his affability and a body so huge that it might have been supposed he came from another planet, like those individuals who have begun to invade our earth the last few years, drew an obscene picture of a couple entwined in a posture that scandalized modesty. In accordance with practice, he asked one of the mischievous students to write under it a particular defective's name. But the student wrote the name of a notorious thug of the district, one of the quarter's biggest troublemakers. As soon as the latter set eyes on that, he grabbed the idiot by the back of the head and swore he would make him erase the signature with his tongue. The idiot resisted heroically, and a fight broke out between the two men. A crowd quickly gathered round, some of them cheering the idiot on to knock out his opponent, while others cheered for the well-known thug. The more rational sector of the quarter — and how many they were! — kept repeating: "There is no power or might except in God" and advising the two opponents to let reason be the arbitrator!

But how, I ask you, can an idiot comply with reason?

The problem was not resolved until another idiot volunteered to lick off the writing, on condition that the accused pay him a couple of *halalas*, the price of a glass of soaked-raisin juice that was sold as a cold drink before the introduction of carbonated drinks.

One of the celebrities of the quarter at the time was an idiot who was doubly blessed, for he was also blind. He was known among us as "the bomb," since rockets were not known then. The reason for this peculiar name was that, despite his blindness, he walked with great speed, holding his stick in front of him in such a way that he collided with everything: people, animals and especially those vendors who displayed their wares in a long row in the middle of al-Tafran Square.

Whenever he bumped into obstacles or people, he would shout out as loudly as he could, "What's this? Are you blind?" He would say this to objects, people and animals alike, then proceed on his way, veering to right or left according to the position of the particular thing with which he had collided. Although he was frequently bruised or cut as a result of these accidents, his habitual behavior never changed. He most probably lacked the early warning system built into most human beings. He disappeared from the quarter only after running into a donkey belonging to one of the elite of the quarter. It was not only the accident itself which led to his disappearance, but also what happened after it. It would appear that the donkey decided to quarrel with its antagonist, who in turn almost bit off the creature's ear. The donkey's owner lodged a complaint with the corporal at the police station, who escorted the offender to the local asylum and had him locked up. That was the last we heard of him.

Had we possessed a news agency or a press at the time, this true story would have been considered a noteworthy news item. It isn't an everyday occurrence to come across a man who bites a donkey. This brings to mind a parallel story that we had news of, concerning a Reverend Minister who bit a dog, an incident considered to be topical, in contrast to the possibility of the dog biting the Reverend.

Despite the occasional unfortunate incidents that broke out among the idiots, their relationship with the quarter and its inhabitants was largely friendly. They represented an integral part of the daily routine of the quarter. Indeed, some of them provided its entertainment, and they were responsible for creating our first musical troupe. They did this by improvising with empty barrels and tin cans which had originally contained imported liquids. Every afternoon they would gather in the square and beat those barrels with sticks.

When this group of three felt the need to diversify, they formed a circus troupe and engaged in sports and exercises. They would lift each other up, one above the other. Then, when the three were standing erect, the top one would exclaim, "May God make him victorious," whatever that meant. The laughable part of the feat — if it could be considered humorous — was that the job of lifting was not done logically, that is, with the strongest supporting the other two, but the other way round, with the strongest on top! They were really crazy! No sooner was the show over than the one at the bottom would scream as loud as he could, threatening the two who had stood on his back.

It seems he secretly enjoyed carrying one or the other of them in individual exhibitions that had no connection with the group program. He would often carry them in succession from the square to the well, a distance of almost a hundred meters, breaking into a run if he could, and considering his safe arrival at the well without falling down a triumph. If he arrived otherwise, he would regard it as a defeat for the rider. They were amazing, those idiots!

But their services were indispensable. No one, for instance, was ever unable to fulfill a vow. The idiots were always there to attend a votive feast; they took the alms at the breaking of the Ramadan fast, and they ate the leftovers of wedding and funeral receptions. People used them to transport things, such as bags of rice or boxes of tea. The only things they were prohibited from carrying were wedding furnishings, either from fear of their safety, or due to superstitions surrounding them. The merchants also made use of their services to bring news of their fellow rivals. "Has so and so more customers than I?" they would ask, or "Has he got goods left over or not?" They were also employed for deliberate sabotage, proving that international terrorism and blackmail are deep-rooted in human nature.

The two most notable sabotage projects carried out in our time were connected with two new vendors who had moved into our quarter from another, threatening the local merchants with unfair trade rivalry and eventual ruin. The injured parties employed two of the idiots to eliminate this menace. One was consigned to walk behind a vendor carrying a tray full of yoghurt and cream, until they arrived at the dark narrow bottom of Saqifat al-Safa, where the idiot pinched the man, causing him to lose his balance. All of his wares came crashing down on the ground, breaking most of the yoghurt dishes and ruining the contents. The idiot stood a few steps away repeating: "There is no might or power except in God," and advising the vendor not to return to this quarter, as it was inhabited by *afareet* and jinn.

The second incident occurred when one idiot, prompted by another vendor, threw a pail of dirty water into a deep frying pan full of hot oil, ready for frying *maqliyya,*a popular food Meccans ate at suppertime.

That was the first time I saw an adult cry in agony over the loss of part of his capital or probably all of it. The confluence of the oil and dirty water ruined everything, including the dough prepared for that evening.

The incident was successful in making the vendor return to his own district, leaving the local salesman alone in the field. He thus deprived the quarter of the benefits of competition between tradesmen in keeping with the maxim, "When the horses compete, the riders are happy."

XX

At this time, the now popular phenomenon of the inferiority complex had not yet entered the ambience of our thought. Therefore we could not argue that those idiots were afflicted with a specific complex. However, since everything has a cause, research and investigation carried out by me has made it clear that they were all afflicted with what one might call a poverty complex.

One of the idiots who suffered from one of these complexes, which I will call the *raushan* complex, was possessed of a poetical turn of mind, and he loved to sing and repeat folk songs. His most renowned folk song, with which he saddened the quarter, was: "If I die, bury me next to a *raushan.*" The *raushan* was a mark of prestige. As a building grew in height so its *raushan* multiplied, and a corresponding excitement grew amongst those idiots obsessed with this *raushan* complex. It is common knowledge that the poor and underprivileged usually live in humble dwellings containing only one story with one or two rooms. No one knows if it was what lay behind those latticed windows that caused the complex or the *raushan* itself, with its wood and ornamental engravings, its ostentation, an artifact which along with so many other facets of our culture has disappeared.

Despite the fact that almost everyone breakfasted on *fool,* or cooked dry fava beans, the *fool* complex also existed in our quarter. Its chief proponent was a strapping, muscular young idiot. He came each morning to the *fool* seller in the quarter, who had set up a long wooden table outside his shop. In front of it, he had lined up a number of small, very low stools on which his clients would sit. When the table was almost full, the idiot would arrive, carrying under his arm a warm loaf that one of the bakers was in the habit of donating to him each morning. As soon as he got to the table with the aroma of appetizing food emanating from it, he would break off a piece of bread and try passing it over the first eater's plate at a height of a meter or so. Then, breaking off another piece, he would pass it over the second, the third, and each in succession.

Although no one suffered harm from this aerial performance, many of the customers, annoyed by this particular idiot, would yell and scream at him while the idiot persistently implored: "Just one bite for God's sake." He appeared to be intoxicated with this manner of savoring the essence of food, a habit which he had perfected and pursued daily without interruption.

Had we possessed at this time one-tenth of the field researchers that exist today, they could have documented the social phenomenon of poverty complexes, before they became a thing of the past and our idiots institutionalized, so that we no longer lived a communal life in which they shared.

Doubtless a certain mental disorder in such people is at the bottom of changing their relationships, and is responsible for altering colors and shapes. Accordingly, their perception changes, and they see in people and things what we others do not see, thus rendering their judgment of matters different from ours.

There used to be a flabby, middle-aged negro woman with protruding teeth living in the quarter. Yet each time she happened to pass one of the retarded, he would exclaim: "What rosy cheeks, how lovely you are. Love has made you like this."

Who knows? Perhaps the idiot's sense of time was different from ours. He may in his altered conception of time be able to see things through a longer period than the moment we see them in. It's quite possible that fifty years earlier the negress was endowed with charm and rosy cheeks when she · was young. While it was invisible to our eyes, it might have remained in some place only idiots could detect.

This may account for why in the past, and indeed up until fifty or sixty years ago there was a tendency to confuse madness with goodness, and mysticism with mental disorder. How often have we treated the simple as though they were God's children, seeking a blessing from them, and asking for the charity of their prayers for some reason or other?

XXI

Doubtless the seed or writing that took root in me unawares, and whose first fruits were those precious proverbs, had begun to develop silently and imperceptibly. I was fascinated by the idea of writing a long story or novel modeled on some of the translated novels I had read. But what should I write about? Every novel I had read had one or more heroes, and likewise one or more heroines. How could I invent heroines when I had never seen a female. To my way of thinking, Mother and Auntie Asma weren't females. How could I understand how women thought or acted? Certainly my thorough knowledge of the feminine ending in desinential inflection[37] didn't help to make me more knowledgeable of them. After giving the matter much thought I decided first of all to look for a title for my projected story, then search for a subject and characters. Eventually, I hit upon what sounded like a promising title—*Rooftop Nights.* I considered those moments and hours I spent on the roof of our house to be the most poetic of my life, nearly all of them having been spent peacefully in the company of the brilliant stars in the quiet of the night. Little by little the embryonic shape of the hero began to take form in my mind and then on paper. He was an adolescent of such sensitivity that the light of the full moon almost made him lose his reason. The seed gestated so rapidly that I filled page after page, surprising myself by such progress. Where had all those emotions come from, that filled this young man's soul? And what had enabled me to imagine his life, since no thought of him had ever occurred to me before commencing this novel. By the time I had completed the first chapter, I was convinced that the maxim about poetry, "The sweetest poetry is the most false," could be applied to other forms of writing as well.

But I was only beginning, and, no sooner had I finished that chapter, than I received the second lesson in the life of a writer: you cannot write whenever you wish, but only when inspiration is with you. Unfortunately, it was to be several years before I was similarly inspired.

Amazed at what I had written, I decided to take my manuscript to *Ustadh* Umar, hoping thereby to heal the rift that had opened between us. I felt confident that no matter what his opinion about the quality of the writing was, he could not say: "There's nothing original in it." I was hopeful he'd find something else to say.

I went back to see him after a number of days of anticipating disappointment. But he gave me a pleasant smile, not that faint smile he would leave on his lips for a long time, and to which I had grown accustomed. This time he got up when he saw me, something he had never done before. Upon returning my papers with suitably encouraging words, he handed me one of his books in which he had written an esteemed dedication to the outstanding young man, Muhaisin, upon the occasion of his first literary creation. This was a surprise I had not dreamed of on setting out that day. The most I had hoped for was to have my papers returned without having a death sentence pronounced on them. That he would both accept my work and praise it had never entered my head, let alone the idea of his accompanying such praise with the gift of a personally inscribed book.

I worked hard to add other chapters to my initial success in an effort to complete the story in some way or other, but to no avail. It was a rooster's egg, an only child without sister or brother. Every time I met the *Ustadh*, he would ask: "Where's the rest?" I would smile and say: "On the way," but what a struggle that was to be!

A few weeks later I forgot *Rooftop Nights* completely, and the illustrious young man did not become the writer the *Ustadh* had predicted.

However, my visits to him continued without interruption; and those occasions I spent with him during my last year of study were the highlight of the day.

On one of my visits he proposed that I should give Arabic language lessons to his son, Jameel. Quite unprepared for his suggestion, I replied: "And you will give me English language lessons in return?"

I can't imagine how I conceived of this idea, nor how I had been able to answer more swiftly than a computer. Doubtless a person's brain has two parts: a part that acts according to reason, and a part that responds to its own desires. I think this is the origin of the folk proverb: "So and so has two minds." They mean by this that he has ideas and ways of doing things that don't usually occur to people.

His mouth gaped open so spontaneously that I was overjoyed. He may have been expecting me to make a show of declining out of modesty, after which he would press me, I would excuse myself, he would ask again, and finally I would accept saying: "I can't guarantee the results but I'll try." Or he may have expected me to hold my silence, allowing him to say: "And I'll give you a Turkish *majidi* every month." He probably expected one of these responses. Indeed, he may have prepared himself for a dozen different answers, but he certainly wasn't prepared for the spontaneity of my response.

I don't imagine that anyone in our quarter was aware that the English language existed; and the few who may have known of its existence attached no importance to it, firstly because it was the language spoken by the Christians, and secondly because it was a useless language. If it had been of any use, the Meccans would have pursued it, for they were renowned for their ability to learn different languages — a gift that was common to me also. I was conversant with words in many of the languages introduced by pilgrims, and to this day I can count in Hausa, the language of the Nigerian people.

I continued staring at him, exhilarated by what I had done. This only served to increase his bewilderment. He decided to say something, but he faltered. I considered this a great personal victory. In the end he simply said: "Agreed." "I'll teach your son three days a week," I prompted, "and you can teach me three. On Fridays we'll both rest." He nodded his head. So we began.

His son, Jameel, was a fellow classmate of mine in our local school. He was the young fellow who had caused Sufyan to be dragged to al-Safa prison, where they spat on him. Yes, he was a fellow student, but not one that would ever set the world on fire or attract people's attention. He didn't even have the ability to make the slightest ripple in the world.

To tell you the truth, the age was not aware of his existence. It is only now that the *Ustadh* has left this world for another, that I can dare to say that Jameel was what we call a bit dimwitted. No one could understand how a man of the *Ustadh*'s intelligence could have so opposite a son. Perhaps the reasons were hereditary, as when a fair-skinned camel gives birth to a black one. Or is it the application of the principle of reverting to the mean average that psychologists claim happens whenever an exceptionally clever man marries a brilliant woman? Instead of their offspring being endowed with greater intelligence than the parents, they

61

are given less. If this were the case, then Jameel had reverted to the mean average, inclining toward backwardness.

Naturally, I didn't teach him *al-Alfiyya* of Ibn Malik. How could I, when he couldn't tell the difference between the word for a stick, *al-asa* and the verb to disobey, *asa*. When I finally got it into his head that there was something in the world called a noun, and something else called a verb, he insisted that, in the structure "the boy is being quick," the word *quick* was a verb and the subject was *being*. No one, not I, the *Ustadh*, nor the boy's mother, who arrived veiled when she heard us shouting, could convince him otherwise. *Ustadh* Umar's ears turned red, and Jameel's mother implored us to accept his wrong idea in return for his accepting another idea in the next lesson. My ears grew red also in the effort to make her understand that a noun is a noun and a verb a verb, and to know this was paramount. But she just said: "It is all God's work." When my arguments failed, *Ustadh* Umar withdrew to his study, leaving me with the still unresolved problem that had become more thorny than before.

It didn't take us long to realize that we were both losers in this bargain. The *Ustadh* had obligated himself to do something against his will, for the number of words and sentences I had memorized exceeded what he had expected, while Jameel was still jogging on the same spot, forgetting today what he had learned the day before. *Umm* Jameel would repeat: "There is no power or might except in God," because she thought I wasn't treating him according to his mental ability. He began to grow more obdurate with each lesson. One day he would agree that *in* was a preposition, then change his mind, insisting it was a noun, qualifying his argument by saying that, when we ask "Is so and so in the house?" we say *in* meaning *present*.

Despite the fact that I would leave *Ustadh* Umar's house with my head reeling, I kept up the endeavor. Naturally the reason wasn't a desire for the promulgation of knowledge, so much as it was a wish to acquire it in a language known in our quarter only by the *Ustadh* and myself in the future.

I found myself rapidly advancing like someone afraid to miss an opportunity that may never come his way again. Jameel's progress was contradictory: one step forward and one back. Although I succeeded after a few months in coming to terms with him on a list of words, insofar as it became common knowledge between us that a certain word was a verb, another a noun, and still another a preposition, he would from time to time reconsider the matter and dispute the truth of what I had taught him. However, prepared in advance for this, I would show him the pages on

62

which he had written that word in his own handwriting, conclusively determining its classification, and then there could be no retracting from what had been established.

Feeling that the *Ustadh* intended to renege on the agreement he had made with me, I took the precaution of drawing up a counter strategy. Reviewing the extent of Jameel's knowledge, together with the sentences he could parse, I contrived by mutual agreement to invite the *Ustadh* to one of our lessons. During this lesson I questioned Jameel about certain words, inwardly praying to God to save the situation and imploring Him not to have the Freemason intrude and ask Jameel questions about words whose classification was still being disputed. Fortunately, all went according to plan, and, after asking Jameel to return to the room we used for a study, I endeavored to ascertain what impression we had made on the *Ustadh*.

Raising his head, the *Ustadh* said: "I would never have believed anyone could convince Jameel the way you have." There was a pause before he continued: "I asked you to give him these lessons, having myself failed to advance his education. It would seem that both of you being almost the same age has something to do with the nature of your success."

Whether the disparity in age between father and son was the cause of his failure or not, I knew now for certain that I would be able to continue teaching and being taught for some months to come.

XXII

Muhaisin's connection with that school terminated at the end of the year, or so he thought, when he graduated with the highest certificate attainable at the beginning of the fourteenth century *Hijri*.[38] At the customary school ceremony prizes were awarded to the outstanding students and certificates to the graduates together with wishes for their success in future careers. The ceremonies were interspersed with speeches and dramatics consisting of an academic debate between Knowledge and Ignorance, which invariably resulted in the triumph of Knowledge, despite the hypotheses ventured that the ignorant were superior in their freedom from anxiety and their natural enjoyment of life, while, in contrast, the learned were made miserable by their knowledge. The drama ended with the debate: "Are they equal — those who know and those who do not know?"[39] And Ignorance, unable to draw on a holy verse to substantiate its argument, was silenced.

I had thought that this would be the last day I would see the school in which I had spent six whole years of my life. How wrong I was to be proven! No sooner had the ceremonies ended and the guests begun to file out of the hall, than the principal came toward me, pointing his finger at me and saying: "Boy, boy." His manner had me assume he was addressing someone else. How could I still consider myself a boy after the eulogies delivered about that year's graduates in the ceremony? However, as he kept on pointing at me, I could do nothing else but step toward him. When I came up to him, he said: "I want to speak to you about an important matter. Come to my office tomorrow morning."

The next morning I slept as late as I wished, conscious of the pleasure of leisure, and my not having to get up at a certain time to rush off to school before the doorman closed the gates. Mother's way of contributing to my celebration was to prepare *areeka* with her own hands, drowning it in a cup of genuine goat butter. She also lit a small fire in the brazier, on which she placed some delightful incense whose fragrance I can still smell whenever I recall that day. When I made a move in the late morning to go out and see the principal, she put a very small, round, mysterious packet in my pocket, saying: "May God protect you from the evil eye."

In the principal's room the boy—I—advanced as he motioned me to be seated. I sat down. After inviting me to drink a cup of tea with him, he said: "There is a current vacancy for a teacher in the school, and I have decided to award you the appointment, as I believe you are suitable for the job." After telling me that the salary for the post was ten *majidi* a month, he remained silent.

I stared at him and the cup of tea in my hand, like someone seeing things with clarity for the first time in his life. What a strange creature I was! I had given no forethought to what I should do after completing my studies. I had never felt it to be a matter of concern. Why should I? All my needs were abundantly supplied: two new gowns and new shoes at feast times, school copybooks, a daily allowance. Mother provided everything at the right times. My breakfast and dinner were prepared for me, so it was understandable that I shouldn't be unduly concerned about the future.

"Why don't you say something?" he said as I continued staring into space. I almost replied: "Allow me to consult my mother first." However, as I didn't reply, he repeated the question: "Speak . . . say something. Are you mute?"

On the spur of the moment I replied: "I'm not a boy, so please don't call me one!" He behaved with me as he had done on our first meeting, looking round to left and right, remarking: "I say one thing and he replies with something quite the opposite!"

"Please," I said. "You don't address the other teachers as boy, but as *ustadh, shaikh*, the father of so and so, or *mawlana*, so why am I the exception, and the only one of God's creatures you refer to as boy, and embarrassingly so in front of people?" Clapping his hands together, he remarked: "There is no might or power except in God. Boys these days are impossible!" Then he went on to say: "Muhaisin, my son, you are younger than my own boys." "You may call me son," I replied, "that's perfectly acceptable, but never boy." "Fine, son," he continued, "now let us discuss the position I am offering you." "I've hardly had time to consider such a matter," I replied. "I fancied I would not have the occasion to see this room ever again after yesterday, and here you are tying me to it. You must give me time to picture myself in this new position." "To picture yourself?" he asked with an air of incredulity. "And what do you mean by that? Here I am offering you the opportunity to join the teaching staff and, instead of expressing gratitude, you ask for time to picture yourself taking up the post!"

Sensing that this dispute was leading nowhere, I said: "It's agreed." Continuing to look round again, he repeated the word "Agreed?" "What is this expression 'agreed'?" he queried. "My proposal was not one of whether you were willing or not to aspire to the position." "I value your patronage" was my reply, to which he said: "At last you're talking." Pouring me a second cup of tea, he proceeded to instruct me in my future role. "As from tomorrow," he said, "the school doors will be closed, and will not open again until the time of the second round of examinations. You must provide yourself with a cloak and a turban, and report to the vice-principal or his assistant every day following the afternoon prayer in the mosque. He will give you instructions and advice on teaching methods and how to deal with the students. It's important that you should study this book," and he gave me a book he had in his hand. "You will be expected to teach Arabic grammar and literary texts. And to provide you with practical training, I have arranged with fathers of various students who did not pass the examinations for you to give those students special lessons.

They will gather at the Dareeba Gate, where there is a recessed room owned by one of the parents. After you have said the evening prayer, you will go there to begin their instruction, starting the day after tomorrow and. . ."

He continued for a long time to outline the schedule he had laid down for me. "They will give you a *majidi* monthly, and if the boys succeed, each father will give you an additional *majidi*. When school resumes, God willing, after the month of Ramadan, visit me at my home, so I can examine you in the material you will be teaching. And always bear in mind, Muhaisin, that students fall into three categories..."

He went on for a whole hour talking to me about the students and their problems and the difficulties entailed in school administration. After I had listened to him, I changed my opinion of his character: he wasn't naive, he wasn't simple-minded, nor was he boorish. At the end of the interview, I actually kissed his head as he had wished, causing him to say with a smile: "I have gained a fourth son today."

XXIII

The house which Father had left us in the Ajyad Quarter was a simple dwelling with nothing noteworthy about it. To us, however, it was everything in the world. We lived in it, or in part of it, throughout the year, renting out most of the house during the pilgrimage season. This enabled my mother and me to live quite comfortably on the rent, self-sufficient and happy within our means.

The house comprised several rooms whose interrelationship is not easy to describe. This was in part due to the shape of the land on which the house was built, which resembled those of the other adjoining lots. The land was an elongated strip, no more than six meters wide by the street door, but continuing on to a depth of thirty meters or more. Thus, on first entering the house, one found oneself in a long dark corridor. A little distance to the left was a door giving on to a sitting room, or reception room for guests, a square room not larger than four by four meters. This contained a small water closet with a water faucet attached to a plastered container. Then a limited space was occupied by the large Moroccan water-jar, which was the most valuable item in the house and the most useful.

If one progressed a little further along the corridor, one came to another door, which opened onto an anteroom connecting the aforementioned sitting room with a family room, a kitchen and a pantry. From this anteroom one could climb up to the first rooftop and find oneself in the main bedroom of the house. It was an odd room in comparison with today's standards, since it had no roof or walls. Its only furniture consisted of three benches, bare by day and furnished at night with bedding which we rolled up in the morning and placed in a corner covered by a tin roof. There was nothing else visible there except four nails fixed in the cormers, used for tying the cords of the now almost obsolete mosquito net, which protected us from the squalls of mosquitoes that hummed around us all night long. This part of the house was the section we used for most of the year until the pilgrims arrived, and then we relinquished it under terms of rent.

Moving through another portion of this spacious house, one discovered sunlight filtering into the corridor, since this part was not roofed over. From here one followed the corridor to an alcove for coal and came upon another living room, another small, open space, and a second alcove for rabbits. This section of the house constituted our living quarters during the pilgrimage season when the house was rented.

The third and last section of the house was an elevated sitting room to which one ascended at the end of the long corridor. It was a bright room with its own rooftop and a water closet. Behind the room was a small, open space where, if one went out, one found oneself surrounded by the dominant mountain range of the Seven Girls, with dwellings scattered along its slopes.

We raised hens in that open space, despite our battle with a fox which came nightly from the mountain to raid the chicken run. In its cunning, it would dig a small hole just large enough to insert one of its paws and grab the first chicken which it came into contact with. On numerous occasions we found the gutted remains of a hen lying among the live chickens. The chickens learned nothing from the victim's struggle, and remained unaware that every inmate of the pen was a nominee to become the next night's casualty.

Our victory over that wily fox was not easily accomplished; but in the end, due to a masterly course of action devised by Mother, both in its small detail and in its overall strategy, we were finally able to terminate its incessant depredations. The gist of this plan, for the benefit of anyone plagued by foxes, was to dig a trench twenty centimeters wide and thirty deep, and to fill it in with water. The trench was covered with a thin piece of plywood and dusted with a fine layer of dirt so that it was indiscernible.

67

The trap was laid close to that part of the pen where the fox gained access. The object, naturally, was to have the fox fall into the trench when it stepped over it on the way to its prey. This is exactly what happened, and we found the creature the next morning drowned in a handspan of water. The gradual depletion of our hens and their "sweet voiced" rooster ceased after the fox's death.

But even then their safety was not totally assured, and several times the *shawta* pestilence decimated our "national resource" taking off most of them as the bubonic plague does humans. However, we did take some precautionary measures against this disease and were able to treat those victims endowed with stronger constitutions. The weak ones, on the other hand, died almost instantly, in keeping with the principle of "the survival of the fittest."

When the pestilence was rampant, you would hear one of the hens give a single, protracted squawk and give up the ghost. We would remove the corpse to the alley and leave it as food for the neighborhood dogs and cats. The pestilence might rage for as long as ten days, in the course of which most of the hens died.

During such times we endeavored to counter our losses and restore the coop to its former strength, either by natural or artificial incubation. The first such method was to watch for a hen which began to brood and manifested a desire to incubate eggs. On seeing this, we would give her a clutch of eggs to sit on, and she would break the shells with her beak when the time came to hatch them. Out of the eggs would come beautifully colored chicks to the great delight of the observer.

Artificial incubation was done by burying a number of eggs in bran, a substance that is probably unknown to the new generation. The bran assumed the role of the brooding hen until the eggs hatched and the fledglings appeared.

Since only one cock is selected to be left with the next generation of hens, the operation of sorting the males from the females took place within a few weeks of birth. As for the remaining roosters, they were transported to "Egg Alley," where they were sold, or else, as soon as their legs had developed and they had become older, they ended up, one after another, in Mother's cooking pot. These are adolescent cocks, who are as troublesome as young teenage boys.

We had several methods of distinguishing the roosters of the new generation. One was by listening for their crow, since the young males possess that faculty from an early age, only their vocals are less developed than in the adults who have become practiced in the art. Another distinguishing feature is the appearance of the cockscomb, something not developed in the female. The third and most complex way of determining a rooster was to grasp the chick by its beak, letting the rest of its body dangle in the air. If it flaps its little wings in a violent, nervous manner, it is without doubt a male.

If science today sees the chicken as a source of food, eggs and feathers, our chickens gave us, in addition to this, folded *mutabbaq* pastries and measures of millet. From the economic standpoint therefore, they represented a natural source of wealth for us. And they did so in quite a simple manner. We usually kept around twenty hens and a rooster. Since statistics, both old and new, have established that the average annual production for a hen varies from two hundred to three hundred eggs, and since there were only two of us, it followed quite logically that we were unable to consume the thousands of eggs that represented our yearly production. Our surplus resulted in our continuous bargaining with Balaqaf on the one hand and *Amm* al-Ashmuni on the other. With the first we exchanged twenty eggs for a half measure of millet, and with the second fifteen eggs for two folded *mutabbaq* pastries, one sweet and the other salty. The latter transaction occurred once every two weeks, according to our own surplus of eggs and the extent of our craving for those pastries famous to all the inhabitants of Amir alley.

XXIV

Mother's loud cry of joy was like a wedding ululation when I returned home to tell her of my appointment as a teacher. She ran to imbibe a mouthful of water and then squirted it over me, this being the custom of the time to prevent one's falling prey to envy, even from those closest to one. She then went on to declare that she was going to have a small party to celebrate the occasion. She asked me to go to Auntie Asma's house to invite her to lunch, then to the house of another lady, whose name I have forgotten, other than that she was from the Turabi family. Then I was to go and perform the noon prayer, with two additional prostrations in thanks to God, while she prepared the food for lunch.

We four dined that day in the principal room of the house. The only factor of surprise was that the mistress of the Turabi family dined with us veiled, in recognition of my having achieved manhood, a formality that enraged Auntie Asma, who exclaimed: "What is the meaning of this? He is still a child — he's younger than your youngest son." But she insisted on maintaining her veil, and the subsequent disquiet in the atmosphere left me embarrassed in the company of the three ladies.

My first days as a teacher were unprecedentedly difficult and tedious. I hardly recognized myself marching along every morning wearing a turban and *jubba*. It would take me several minutes each morning to fix my turban at the appropriate angle, all the time amazed at the sight of the person I saw staring back at me from the mirror. Although Mother insisted that I resembled Father in my new attire, I was certain that I was miscast in my role, and I didn't care for the image I presented. Moreover, I wasn't comfortable or relaxed standing or sitting in front of a group of students. Despite my place in life having changed from a recipient of knowledge to a transmitter of it, I remained deep down inside the student I had been a short time ago.

To make matters worse, the principal insisted on attending my classes for the first few days in order to ascertain my ability in the profession he had chosen for me. He would sit on the floor at the back of the room, listening attentively to every word I said, and would several times indicate with his forefinger that I had made a mistake or committed an unintentional error in grammar. The only benefit I derived from his presence was the quiet that prevailed in the classroom while he was there. No one dared raise his voice or torment his neighbor or disrupt the order of the class. The image of the mischievous Sufyan stood out before me during these lessons, as I tried to figure out who his successor would be in this class, expecting at any moment a *nabaq* seed to come flying at me or one of the students. However, the presence of the principal was sufficient guarantee that nothing like that would happen.

Sitting in the teachers' room was no more conducive to my peace of mind than being in the classroom. All these teachers had been my professors, and I was not used to sitting and conversing with them. I would therefore remain silent in their company. As soon as the control officer's whistle announced the beginning of the next lesson, I would be the first to get away to the classroom. Thus, my day was spent in scurrying back and forth to the classroom or hurrying home at an equal speed in the hope that no one would see me in my official clothes. I expected at any moment to encounter one of my former mischievous comrades from the quarter, certain that my appearance would meet with a loud guffaw, or that sarcastic remarks would be aimed at my person.

One day somebody concealed a neatly folded piece of paper in my cloak pocket. I had no idea of its contents until I reached home and opened it. There I discovered what I had been expecting. The note consisted of a single line of poetry:

When he puts on the turban, he becomes a monkey,
And a pig when he leaves it off.

On reading this, I went into the water closet and burst into tears, in a suppressed voice at first, then in a loud audible wail. This startled Mother, who ran to find out what had happened. I must have cut a strange figure, standing there in that enclosure to which one comes to answer the call of nature, fully dressed and sobbing aloud, with Mother fruitlessly patting my shoulder. My distress prompted her to first take off my turban, then my cloak. She then led me to the rooftop so that I might get a breath of fresh air, as she expressed it, all the while repeating prayers beseeching God's help and strength and His protection from the wiles of the devil. Over and over again, she kept on asking me what had happened, while I was still unable to refrain from tears. When I grew calmer, I felt ashamed of my behavior in front of Mother. What should I tell her? Given her pride in my profession, how could I account for my misery?

As a last resort, I ran to the Holy Mosque, always my refuge in crises, where I began to circumambulate the Kaaba, seven times by seven, until I no longer knew how many full circuits I had completed. After that I had a warm drink from the bucket at the Zamzam[40] Well, until I was so full I felt that my rib cage was about to split open. Only then did I regain my composure. I hurried back home to reassure Mother of my well-being, and things resumed their normal course.

At the same time I endeavored to rationalize the situation and conjecture about who could have placed that piece of paper in my pocket. In my mind I went over the events preceding my discovery of the note. I reviewed the exit from class after the last period, the crush at the door, the milling students, and one whose face leaped out before me, making for me, and pushing the others out of the way. Yes, he was the culprit—none else. But why?

I engaged in a retrospective of my life at the school over six years, recalling how we had been in the same class in our first year. He had dropped behind to repeat the year, while I graduated to the second year's study, and I hadn't seen him again until, without warning, he had appeared before me. I wondered what year he was in now, and decided to find out. But, in the meantime, I had to decide on a strategy for the next day. I had to meet him again, and I debated whether or not to report him to the principal, or summon him to the teacher's common room to explain his behavior and upbraid him. Would I be able to do that? I could almost see myself shaking with fear of him as a consequence. And, to make matters worse, the thing would become known to the rest of the staff, and I would be forced to read the line of poetry to them. What if one of them were to burst out laughing in front of the offending student? That would embarrass me further.

No, I told myself, that's not the way to handle this affair. I would have to resort to the method whose principles I had learned from experience, namely one of strategy and planning. The first strategic maneuver I had assimilated over the long years was to try and disguise my intended actions by pretending to do something else. In keeping with that principle, I forced myself to smile warmly when I met the fellow the following day during the few minutes between classes. I even patted him on the shoulder, as an experienced person might someone younger—although he was older and broader than me—and stretched out my hand toward his ear with the endearment of a father to his naughty child, saying: "Are you still up to mischief?" I then inquired in a friendly manner as to what school year he was in, since I hadn't seen him for a number of years.

"I'm in the second year of the advanced section," he replied to my question.

"Then," I said, "next year, when you have completed your studies, I shall recommend your appointment as a teacher, and I shall correspondingly place that piece of paper in your pocket." He hung his head with shame, while I left him and went on my way. Those few moments of confrontation had so exhausted me that I felt, when I entered the teacher's room, like someone who has survived hand-to-hand combat with a giant or a wild animal.

XXV

No sooner had the principal ceased to attend my classes than all chaos set in, with the students shouting aloud and generally tormenting one another. Every day presented a new problem, and I tried to combat the situation by following the advice which the principal had initially given me at the time of my appointment. I attempted to classify the students according to his three categories. But what worsened my predicament was my relationship with the other members of the staff, as I was unable to establish an affinity with them, or act as if I were one of them.

The situation grew to be so intolerable that I went to see the principal and asked him to assign me to an administrative task instead of teaching. He refused, however, on the grounds that the school didn't need any additional administrators. He asked me to talk about my difficulties, in the hope that he might be able to help me overcome them.

"It's the staff," I said, "I don't feel that I am one of them."

"That's only natural to begin with," he replied, adding that there was a periodic luncheon at one or another of their homes. He assured me that he would invite me to his house the following week, where I would be able to socialize with some of the faculty outside the atmosphere of school. His suggestion proved to be a good one, giving further evidence of the measure of wisdom and expertise he possessed.

I was thus enabled to discover the difference between a person with his head covered and uncovered, a theory which over the years has come to constitute for me a general rule, regardless of whether the person is inclined to wear a turban, a fez, or a foreigner's hat. This principle has been corroborated on numerous occasions, for certainly these teachers were not the same people bare-headed on these occasions as they were when wearing their turbans at work. They exchanged wisecracks and jokes, even making fun of one another with amusing anecdotes, true or fictitious. The purpose of the dinner was relaxation, to ensure that they did not become psychologically exhausted and narrow-minded, as had various of their predecessors, who had grown inflexibly serious.

When the food was served, they tossed a certain organ of the sheep to each other several times, and ended by burying it beneath the layers of rice which supported the entire lamb.

The only person not to participate in these antics was *Mawlana*, who alone held this title. *Mawlana* was tall and stout, with such an expression of dignity that one could scarcely look at him. Although he wouldn't condescend to join in our harmless amusement, he did take off his turban along with the others, thereby affording his naturally austere face a greater humanity.

I found myself able to join in the general merriment of this small Meccan company. I wasn't too timid to relate an amusing story to one or another of them, or to supply an anecdote making fun of an action similar to his. I even went so far as to cut off the sheep's tongue, placing the larger part of it in front of *Mawlana*, who regarded me with a smile, then duly ate the tongue without showing a flicker of anger or annoyance.[41]

It seems reasonable to suppose that headgear and clothes generally hide a good deal of a man's inner self and the nature of his personality, as well as serving to disguise his physical shape. Moreover, the kind of clothes and the amount of starch in them all contribute to the deception of people's appearance. The falsity of appearance created by clothes may well account for the custom of the ancient Chinese, who, noted for their wisdom, declared thousands of years ago: "If you want to get to know a man, talk with him in his nightclothes," that is, in his pyjamas. The reason for this is that a person is likely to be truer to himself, and less affected at such a time, than when he is wearing official costume. When a man is dressed up, he admires his mirror image and likewise remembers his social position or his wealth, and behaves according to these two factors, not according to what he feels.

The Europeans, especially in northern Europe, have taken a step forward or backward with regard to the maxim about nightclothes, having discovered that the best relationships and deals are reached in a sauna where people remove not only their headdress, but also everything else. The scantiest of covering is worn by the most conservative among them, while the others are content to let mere steam cover them.

To return to the subject of headwear, one might mention that it was an old custom to say that so-and-so had "uncovered his head," meaning that he had disclosed his true intentions. Most probably, the phrase was used to indicate that someone had dropped all consideration and reservation. They used to say of a woman who openly revealed her desires, that she had unveiled her face, since the female head covering was a veil, not a turban. Nowadays you will observe a European man raising his hat when he greets a lady, in token of his respect or feelings toward her. Likewise, when he visits another person at home, he takes off his hat as soon as he enters, as if to state: Here I am without concealing anything.

The common folk used to say: Better to lose one's head than one's turban, meaning that the removal of the latter stripped its owner of his halo and revealed him to others as he really was. As a consequence of this dinner at the headmaster's house, I was so excited about the revolution that had occurred in my relations with my colleagues and the genuine baring of our heads, that I suggested to the principal that I invite them all to my place the next Friday. His advice was: "Don't rush things or invite anyone until you have eaten in all of their homes first; then it will be your turn." Naturally, I obeyed, and was later convinced of the accuracy of his judgement, when the other members of the staff began to press me to organize the next Friday luncheon at my home or to arrange one for the following week. I answered their impulsiveness by saying: "Whoever gives on Saturday will receive on Sunday. Most of you haven't extended an invitation yet, so what right have you to make this demand on me?"

XXVI

The ample salary I received from the school created an economic problem in itself, as it gave rise to what is known as a cash surplus or an imbalance in the budget. I had to give constant consideration to various ways of spending this money, or at least a portion of it. It's even possible that the future inflation crisis was a direct consequence of people like myself whose income had suddenly multiplied. I was visibly perturbed when I received my monthly salary, not knowing what to do with it. Where should I put it? How could I hide it? Naturally Mother offered the best possible guidance in financial matters. She would take the ten riyals from me as I stood there in silence and, closing her hand quickly upon the money, race to the farthest room to hide it in a safe place.

Mother also thought of ways to improve our standard of living. Her first move in this respect was to employ the services of one of the "African" women who used to walk around the streets of Mecca calling out: "We'll wash the dishes and sweep the stairs." She employed one of them to do precisely this, on a daily or weekly basis as required. As a consequence, the hallway became thoroughly clean. Similarly, in contrast to its previous condition, the sitting room in the upper part of the house was maintained ready for the reception of pilgrims. In time she came to give additional tasks to these energetic workers, entrusting them with washing the clothes every Tuesday, because it was on that day, according to popular tradition, that the mountains were created. The directions that Mother laid down for *faqeeha*, as these African women were called, were that Mother would herself prepare the washtub by filling it with plenty of ash and then water, and then leave the wash to soak. Since washing detergents were still unknown, ashes were used to remove stains and dirt in an effective and practical manner. The *faqeeha* undertook the first two washes, which were the most laborious part of the operation, while Mother reserved for herself the last, to which she added starch or bluing as required.

It would be wrong to assume that our relation with the *faqeehas* began only at that time. The truth is that in earlier centuries every family employed them. Who else would have pounded the wheat for the soup favored by Meccan families, which constituted the main dish during the month of Ramadan? That operation was performed each year in the latter half of the month of Shaaban,[42] when these women would go out into the streets of Mecca carrying wooden mortars of perhaps a meter in height, crying out, "We'll pound the soup wheat." The women of the quarter would then hasten to call them in and bargain over the fee required for the task. It was all carried out in an orderly fashion, despite the fact that, according to rumors spread in those days about them, those African women belonged to the Namnam tribe, who were cannibals. The rumor was verified by the existence several centuries later of the Emperor Indasa, who demonstrated the practicalities of cannibalism when he cooked and ate one of his ministers for lunch before the minister should eat his Emperor for dinner.

As a result of the extra help she received, Mother enjoyed a good deal of leisure time which she had to occupy in some way. She either applied herself to her loom for hours, or embroidered our handkerchiefs and drawers, as was the fashion among the notables of our day. She also devoted greater thought to the preparation of our meals, which was evidenced not only in the excellence of the cooking but also in its variety and amount. In turn, this prosperity was reflected in both our figures, with the result that our garments no longer hung loose on us but were molded to the shape of our figures.

Mother's management of household affairs went beyond this to securing a variety of new domestic appliances, utensils and items of furniture.

This was something she did whenever her palm itched, which indicated in common belief that it was time to spend what was in one's pocket in order to make way for what Providence had in store for one.

One appliance which afforded me lasting pleasure was our home ice-cream maker. It was a most useful machine, turned by hand after one had put a quantity of crushed ice into the outer container, and a cup or two of sweetened lemon juice into the inner one. When the juice was almost frozen it became ice cream ready for our consumption.

I am not giving away family secrets when I say that Mother was of a cheerful disposition, crooning to herself all day long in a low voice. In those days her favorite song was the Syrian one: "Shake, shake, O sycamore tree; the apples of Syria are delectably sweet."

The secret I am less willing to disclose is that one day, a long time ago, Mother had purchased a phonograph or "singing box" as it was called then. How she had bought it and from whom was known only to herself. She placed it in the back room and insulated the sound by stuffing rags inside it, anxious that her neighbors should not be a party to her secret. The discovery of this had me realize for the first time that our parents' actions were not necessarily above suspicion. Although her motive was to diffuse a joyful atmosphere in the house, the phonograph itself made me so nervous that I went about most of the time expecting some disaster to happen should someone at school learn of its existence. The only thing which relieved my distress was *Ustadh* Umar's advice that I should not concern myself with the matter, since there was nothing dishonorable associated with owning a phonograph. To reassure me, he confessed that he too owned one, and saw no wrong in it. Even more astoundingly, he offered to loan us some of his records, on the condition that we return them at our leisure. As Mother expressed it, this placed him—that Freemason—in the same class as her, this shy woman—much to her astonishment!

XXVII

I continued giving Jameel his Arabic grammar lessons as before, although I introduced a number of changes to enliven them. I did this with the prior consultation of the *Ustadh*, telling him that I thought we should improve Jameel's ability to read, otherwise he could little benefit from laws of grammar divorced from a practical text. I realized that the best way to encourage Jameel to read was to write him out some of the simple stories I recalled from among the tales my mother had told me up on the roof, under a mosquito net while the insects droned around us. In this way I think I passed on to Jameel a compendium, if not the whole, of a folklore transmitted from one generation to another. The only difference in our case was that the stories were transmitted by a male and not, as was customary, by a female. Time and again Jameel's lower jaw would drop in surprise at the turn of events in these tales. It was a depressing sight, giving the impression of complete idiocy rather than simple-mindedness.

The story which fired his imagination most and made his eyes twinkle with delight was the tale of "The Rabbit Forest," which I invented for him and wrote in his notebook one day when the fountain of my mother's stories had dried up. It was a naive tale about a community of rabbits that lived together in perfect harmony in an isolated forest, until the arrival one day of a dust-colored rabbit to the territory. This rabbit began to sow discord in the colony, inciting one group against another until they began to fight and devour one another, until there was only one survivor. He had become huge, having participated in devouring his comrades, until he no longer looked like one of his species. I ended the story by saying that all of the bulls on this earth are descended from this very rabbit, which is the reason they like to eat clover in the manner of their rabbit forebears.

Jameel was so pleased with my story that he read it many times and memorized it by heart. Taking advantage of his enthusiasm for this "bull-rabbit," I asked him to analyze the words grammatically, and to decide whether "the bull" was definite or indefinite, and whether "the rabbit" was masculine or feminine. I believe that he learned more Arabic grammar during those days than at any other time, largely due to his enthusiasm for the rabbit, and his desire to parse every sentence in which the word occurred.

What I didn't take into account was the possibility of the curious question which Jameel sprung on me one day, namely that if all the rabbits had perished in that battle, then what was the origin of the species which was with us today? After careful thought, I replied that these rabbits were the descendants of a herd of bulls who were overtaken by famine and deprivation until their bodies had shrunk to the size of the rabbits we see today. His delight in the tale was magnified by the addition of this episode.

The *Ustadh* was delighted with the continuous progress he noted in his son, and reiterated his thanks on behalf of my efforts. But his face clouded over with sorrow when Jameel read the story of the rabbits to him, and the cloud darkened when he related orally what happened to the hungry bulls who were reduced to the size of rabbits. It was clear to him that Jameel was not a normal person and that neither my efforts nor those of anyone else could transform his backwardness into a higher level of intelligence. Nonetheless, the *Ustadh* encouraged me to continue, remarking that: "If Jameel should be able one day to read some of the books in this library, he might live as seminormal a life as many others."

One day as I was leaving the room in which I taught Jameel, *Ustadh* Umar stopped me and invited me to join him for a cup of tea. He had arranged this in order to surprise me with the gift of a small book called *Common Expressions in the English Language*. I thanked him for the book and was about to leave when he said: "How I wish that my daughter Jameela were a boy. I would have asked you to tutor her, and that would have been a fruitful experience. She is so very intelligent that it seems as though she has taken both her own and her brother's share of brains."

I thanked him for his concern over the trouble I was taking with Jameel and his worry about the conscientiousness I exerted with such poor results on the part of his son. I didn't give his mention of Jameela a second thought, for I regarded it as his way of showing me his appreciation, and besides, up to a point I enjoyed the lessons I gave Jameel.

However, the subject of Jameela recurred, for *Ustadh* Umar mentioned her on another occasion, saying: "It's unfortunate that there are no schools for girls. It has meant that Jameela has been denied the opportunity of education despite the fact that she deserves it." I asked him why he didn't send her to the Kabariti Kittub for girls, where she could at least learn the *Amma*[43] of the Quran and come to know some of the Quranic chapters, which she could then recite in her prayers. He assured me that he had done this, and that she had learned most of the *Amma* by heart, adding that that was not enough, for she was capable of much more. He lapsed into silence again, and, unsure what to say or do, I also remained silent. Eventually he said: "Were it not for tradition, I would have asked you to give her lessons as you do Jameel." I didn't reply, so he left me to myself and I went home. On my way home I reflected on what he had said about Jameela, and, in the few minutes walking distance that divided our houses, I concluded that the Freemason must have had more on his mind than the mere wish that there should be schools for girls. My suspicions were confirmed a few days later when he asked me: "Isn't learning a duty for all Muslims, men and women?" When I answered in the affirmative, he supported his previous question by saying, "How then can we fulfill this religious duty?" When I did not answer, he asked me point blank, "Would you agree to teach my daughter as you do Jameel?" When I expressed a certain hesitation, he assured me that she would be accompanied by her grandmother and Jameel, of course. I was to divide the lesson between them.

I felt shocked and terrified, but he did not give me a chance to express my inner feelings, for he added, "She will be veiled, of course, and during the first few lessons she will just listen to what goes on between you and Jameel, without participating. That will come later. You may use the same stories and tales which you have written out for Jameel. After she has mastered the art of reading, you can move on to teaching her the school reader which you studied in preparatory school." Then he added, "It is unfair to leave her ignorant when she is capable of acquiring knowledge."

Jameela was younger than both her brother and I, by two or three years. I had not seen her for a considerable period of time, since she was five or six years old. After that she had begun to wear the veil and effectively vanished. In fact, I had entirely forgotten her existence, until her father began talking about her.

In accordance with the principle of "there is no escaping what must be," Jameela attended the first day in the company of her old grandmother, to the great agitation of both her brother and myself. I kept looking around fearing that someone might see us in this situation. The reins were about to slip from my hands when Jameel cried out: "A girl! A girl! How can she be permitted to sit with us in the same place?" To make matters worse, her grandmother kept asking God's pardon in an audible voice, for it appeared that she was not in agreement with the turn of events. She had submitted the matter to God, however, and to the strict orders of the "Free Mason."

Jameela was a strange and unfathomable bundle of whom nothing could be seen, as she was completely covered by a *jama*, a large cloak worn by women which completely enveloped the figure. The only openings in it, from which the wearer could look out on the world, were two small slits for the eyes.

Her body appeared small and slim, unlike the much larger physiques of Jameel and myself. At first she sat in a corner, with her grandmother at her side, and did not make the least movement throughout the course of the lesson. When it was over, she would leave in silence with her grandmother following her, without having once spoken or greeted us.

Then, when the time came for her to participate actively in lessons, *Ustadh* Umar attended in person. He was followed by a boy servant carrying the tea tray and a plate of the cakes which housewives used to prepare during the pilgrimage season. Although *Ustadh* Umar took no part in the class at all, his presence created an atmosphere of confidence and trust that assisted us all, and as a result I insisted that he attend all future lessons. Although he couldn't always attend regularly, he would come in once or twice during the course of class, and assert his presence. The grandmother in time became convinced that what we were doing, while completely unprecedented, represented no great overstepping of boundaries. This conviction was reflected in the greetings which she began to give me whenever she came to the lesson. At first her entry had been marked by silence. Then she began to say, "Peace be upon you," which after a few weeks was expanded to "peace be upon you, son," and in time she grew to exchange a few words with me, asking after my mother, as well as showing admiration for me in my *jubba* and turban. The situation developed to a point whereby she began to ask God to protect me from the evil eye, and finally she went as far as to ask God to reward me generously for the lessons I was giving her grandchildren.

By this time, I was convinced that I had been accepted by the whole family. The clearest confirmation of this was when the *Ustadh's* wife herself attended one of my lessons, and listened to her daughter read one of the stories that I had previously written out for Jameel.

During the time that the grandmother was undergoing the psychological transformation, two other developments were taking place hand in hand. One was Jameela's advancement, for she was really far more intelligent than I had anticipated. She devoured the stories I gave her to read, one after the other. She would, after going through them with me once or twice, review them during the day until she knew them by heart, including the end vowelling, and this without making any grammatical errors, although she was ignorant of the rules of grammar.

The other development took place inside me, for I grew so accustomed to that low voice with its soft resonance that I would miss it during the day and try to remember how it sounded. There was no other clue to her identity, for Jameela had remained an ambiguous, impenetrable screen of clothes, other than that childlike voice which she began to raise little by little as her confidence increased.

At that time, I had not yet read the story "The Love of the Blind," which describes how the blind person, in establishing the growth of love between him and another, begins by depending first on the voice, then secondly on touch. Although I was unfamiliar with the story, I instinctively practiced the principles it related. Having become familiar with her voice, it then began to fascinate me, and I became attached to it without knowing anything of its owner. This inspired me to reread the *diwan* of Majnun Layla,[44] murmuring to myself in my spare moments some of its famous verses such as the one comparing Layla's eyes and neck with those of the gazelle, although it was many years before I was to see her eyes. I wondered at the time about the capacity in a person to become fond of things or people for no other reason than repetition and habit.

Jameela became a mental preoccupation, and I began to draw up a picture of that mysterious slim bundle sitting in front of me, relying for support on the three figures I knew: the grandmother, *Ustadh* Umar and Jameel. I would put this person's nose under that person's forehead, and then add to this Jameel's figure, but making it slimmer, so that a composite image of the veiled girl sitting in front of me took shape in my mind.

The grandmother participated in a practical way in the deepening of my relationship with Jameela's voice. I frequently complained that I could not hear what was being read, whereupon the grandmother would say: "Raise your voice, Jameela, so that Muhaisin can hear you," and added, "He is like your brother and about the same age."

Several months passed without any conversation whatsoever taking place between the teacher and his female student. The amazing progress that Jameela was making, however, required, after consulting with the *Ustadh*, the broadening of the field of knowledge conveyed to her. It was decided, therefore, that I should introduce arithmetic, then grammar. These subjects necessitated the exchange of a few words, followed by questions and answers and discussions in keeping with the maxim—"A greeting leads to conversation"[45]—without ever superseding that barrier.

Jameel no longer complained of his sister's presence, for the pressure formerly concentrated on him was lessened with the division of my time between two pupils. He also grew to enjoy the discussion, and the introduction of questions and answers. From time to time he would even volunteer an answer to a question not addressed to him. He also entered into spirited discussion with his sister, prompting me to take advantage of the opportunity to feed his brain cells, which were beginning to be activated to some degree.

XXVIII

By adopting the turban and cloak, I progressed from childhood and youth to a sedate maturity without having chosen this transition. In this respect, I resembled Steinbeck's heroes in *Of Mice and Men,* who passed from nomadism to degeneracy without going through the intermediate state of civilization.

Even before becoming a teacher and adopting this style of dress, I had never shared in the usual enjoyment of the boys of my generation, in their innocent and not-so-innocent amusements, partly out of fear of being criticized. Nonetheless, I had at least adopted the position of a spectator to the events that occurred around me. How many times had I climbed up the Khandama Ridge, that hill lying at the end of al-Sadd Street, to observe what was going on among the young men of the quarter, whether they were performing the collective dance with sticks called *mizmars* to the bouncing beat of drums or simply mock fighting with sticks, which sometimes turned into duels that grew realistically bloody. These scenes gave me the impression of at least being indirectly involved in the life that went on around me, while not actually participating in it. But I had now renounced all of that forever. How could one devoted to the pursuit of knowledge take pleasure in trivial amusement, despite the fact that his inner feelings remained those of a child and a youth who would have gladly participated in these communal pursuits.

This state of denial also included my abstention from watching the ferocious battles waged between the youths of our quarter and those of the adjacent al-Misfala, whose arena was the Misyal area next to the Mental Hospital, known by virtually all the inhabitants of Mecca, as was its governor, *al-Sayyid* Husain. But, for those unfamiliar with the often hostile relations between the various districts of Mecca at this time, I should briefly outline their diverse relations. Thus, the Shamiyya Quarter was the ally of the Misfala Quarter, the Ajyad Quarter, the ally of the Shubaika Quarter, and both of them sworn enemies of the first two, just as it had been two thousand years ago in the antagonism between various subtribes and among the smaller tribal divisions. On many occasions it was impossible for the people of our quarter of Ajyad to pass through the Misyal area on their way to Lower Mecca to enjoy the clover fields that were abundant there. They would often be attacked by the inhabitants of al-Misfala, unless they should claim to be from a different neighborhood other than the Ajyad Quarter, something that pride and honor rarely permitted. The people of our quarter returned measure for measure, barring the young men of the Misfala Quarter from working in their territory, especially stone cutters who carried stone on the backs of their pack animals from Khandama Mountain to other parts of the city. These clashes followed their own special ritual, beginning with the questioning of the person passing through a particular quarter and inquiring where he had come from and whether he was a friend or enemy. If he proved to be an enemy, he would be requested to return home. If he refused, he had no one to blame but himself in the ensuing fight, one against one. It was a rule followed by both sides that the encounter should be a fair one. The fight ended when one of the contestants was rolled in the dust, his clothes torn and possibly his head bloodied by a stick or a dagger. If the encounter involved two or more of the older generation, it often culminated in the drawing of knives and the evisceration of the weaker of the two contestants. At other times the conflict would take the form of a surprise raid, when a number of combatants would meet and decide to provoke the other quarter in an unrestricted collective attack. This method often resulted in someone being killed or wounded, or both. The matter, however, would be concealed from the authorities, and the victim buried secretly. Plans would then be laid to take revenge on the quarter responsible for the killing, in order to level the score, the initiator being regarded as the more heinous offender.

The most extraordinary story of that era, which one cannot call a "golden era" at all, was that of the waylaying of one of the bullies of the Ma'abda Quarter. Because of his huge size and physical strength, he was called "the Bull"—no one knew his real name. It seems that "the Bull" had assaulted a great many people from the various quarters, beating, stabbing or killing them, a form of behavior that called for a collective revenge. Eventually, three men from Amir Alley agreed to kill him at sunset on a Friday. After praying the afternoon prayer, they made a covenant that no member of the party should retract his commitment or confess the outcome of their pact. Following this, they recited the *Fatiha* over the soul of their adversary "the Bull," on the grounds that he was already as good as dead, and, mounting their donkeys, they headed for the upper part of Mecca on their way to Majarr al-Kabsh at the start of Mina. There they secured their animals to large rocks and squatted down in hiding in readiness for "the Bull" to return from his daily excursion. They confronted him without warning from among the rocks, their staves in their hands. Without any prelude, one of them struck him a blow on the head which knocked him off balance so that he fell to the ground from his donkey's back. Two of them then jumped on his chest and split open his belly as one does with livestock. Having assured themselves that there was no life left in him, they wiped their knives on their clothes, got on their animals and returned to Mecca without anyone being the wiser.

While being deprived of access to certain pleasures in life, I nevertheless acquired other compensations when I moved up the social scale. I became the recipient of invitations to wedding feasts in the quarter, which necessitated one's participation by sending the gift of a sack of sugar or rice, in accordance with the principle that whoever gives on Saturday will receive on Sunday. The custom is, in fact, an excellent one in that all the wedding expenses were covered by the quarter's gifts. And it was not uncommon for the newly married couple to live for a long period on the surplus provided by these wedding gifts, most of which were in the form of nonperishable food supplies, which could be kept for a year or two without spoiling.

It was the accepted custom for the bridegroom to send everyone who had contributed a gift, a tray, or *ma'shara*, full of wedding food and sweets. This tray represented each particular family's provisions for the day, and it was considered a serious violation should any wretch be instrumental in leading the bearer to the wrong house for the consumption of the delicacies. The intended recipients of the gift would thus be left to go hungry, and curse the bridegroom, his family and relatives for their rudeness in failing to carry out their obligations.

I also became a member of our quarter's committee for mediating disputes and restoring well-being, and for assisting the needy whose homes had been destroyed by a flood, or whose furnishings had gone up in smoke. My prestige was facilitated by my increasing weight, the result of abundant food and too little exercise.

According to the dictates of autosuggestion, in which I was proficient, I fancied that I had become a prestigious person not only in our quarter, but in life in general. This so pleased Mother that she often sang ululations when I entered the house, uttering a prayer for protection in the hope that God might shield me from the danger of the envious and the evil eye.

XXIX

The dawn prayer on Friday in the Holy Mosque, or the *Haram*, particularly the *Sajda* [46] created a tremendous spiritual feeling of being lifted up, both for me and many others who lived during that period. This is probably still true for those who live on in Mecca. It was most intoxicating for a man to be able to arrive at the Mosque an hour or so before the call to prayer in order to place his prayer mat in the first row facing the Kaaba. He would then occupy himself with the night-time [47] prayers or in circumambulating the Kaaba, until the *mu'adhdhin* issued the call to prayer. This was all part of an inherited tradition in which sons accompanied their fathers to the Mosque even prior to puberty. Thus they would become habituated to it as their fathers before them, and in turn would pass on the custom to the next generation.

On one of those predawn trips I caught a glimpse of *Mawlana* beneath one of the Mosque porticoes. He was saying the night prayers alone with such lengthy recitation of the Quran that one assumed he would never be finished. I stood watching him from a distance, and, when at last he had finished his prayers, I approached as though I had just noticed him and had to come to pay him my respects. I did, in fact, sit down briefly and greet him, before moving off to the place in which I was accustomed to pray. Though I came to forget the incident, it appears that *Mawlana* did not.

He taught *usul* in the school, that is, the principles of jurisprudence, and also taught the principles of Quranic exegesis, in addition to being an authority on the principles of the Arabic language, or Arabic philology. Strange as it may seem, he also knew something of the Syriac language. He was a pious and respected man, and was said to be a mystic who was the founder of a mystical order whose followers were largely in North Africa. But more than that, it was said that he was endowed with special spiritual powers. Had he lived to these days, this may in time have led to an investigation of his person. If, however, he is still alive, and I don't rule out the possibility, since he was a giant of a man and amazingly strong—he would be well over a hundred.

Not long after the above-mentioned encounter at dawn, *Mawlana* one day invited me home for supper, an invitation which perplexed me, because it was extracurricular to the periodic dinners attended by the teaching staff. It was not an easy task to dine with *Mawlana* alone, since one was at a loss to choose the right topic of conversation. One had to wait until he spoke, or until he showered one with questions. Since he invited me on a second and a third occasion without my ever knowing why, I assumed he had given me his acceptance. On the fourth occasion, he told me that the food we were eating had been prepared by Ameena. Little by little he began to tell me about Ameena, her piety and memorization of the Qur'an, from which he progressed to a physical description of her, while I continued to smile idiotically, in a state of confusion and embarrassment. I realized, after drinking the cups of green tea with which he supplied me, that Ameena was his daughter and that he was offering me her hand. Although he didn't state this openly, his hints were sufficient for me to fear that he would ask me to stretch out my hand, as was the custom, while he said: "I have given her to you in marriage; say that you accept." Instead of doing that, he added by way of comment: "Next time you will see Ameena, since the sight of a woman's face is desirable before marriage, in fact obligatory."

To me, this proposition was like a surgical operation performed on one who was lacking the gift of sight, so that he could be made aware of the existence of things and people. Until that day, I had never thought of getting married nor devoted any consideration to who my lifelong partner might be. And my mother, who took the lead in all important matters, had never so much as raised the subject.

On my way home, the picture of Ameena that had been suggested to me began to take shape in my mind. For some unknown reason, the image of Jameela appeared alongside that of Ameena — the latter very tall, fair-skinned, with a full figure, and the former diminutive, slim and brown, like most Meccan girls of the day. In the short time before reaching home, things became clear to me, as the phantom of Ameena accompanied me through Mecca's dark alleys, so that I could almost touch her with my hand. Her face was not welcoming, but stern, and incorporated a good deal of *Mawland*'s gravity and overpowering personality. By the time I reached home, I was possessed by the fear that this simulacrum might become a reality, with me condemned to live with her for the rest of my life. Mother did not seem surprised at what I told her nor frightened by the idea of my vision.

"What of it," she commented, "fair, tall with a full figure, what more could a man hope for?"

"But I don't want her," I replied.

"You haven't seen her," she said, "so how can you decide?"

"Whether I have seen her or not, the very thought of her beside me terrifies me," I commented.

"Don't turn down God's beneficence."

"What sort of beneficence are you talking about?" I enquired.

"Don't be childish!" Mother retorted. "Instead of being happy when a revered *shaikh* like *Mawlana* offers you his daughter, you get into a state of nerves."

"But I've lived at home quite happily until now, so how can I suddenly live with this Ameena?"

"All men say that at first," she said," but once they've tasted of the nectar, they soon acquire the appetite for more."

"Honey or not doesn't matter. I've never thought about marriage till now and you have never suggested anything like this to me."

"I didn't suggest it because I was afraid of losing you," she said. "I'm alone in the world, but I suppose when one's allotted portion comes along, one shouldn't refuse it."

"When the right person comes along," I replied, "I hope it will be someone else other than Ameena."

"Are you thinking about another woman?" she asked in astonishment.

"Possibly," I replied.

Our discussion, which resembled a dialogue between two deaf persons, went on until I was worn out. In the course of it, I became aware of something for the first time, namely that if my "allotted portion" was unavoidable, I wanted it to be Jameela. It was her that I visualized standing before me, and not that colossal phantom. I was attracted to her and repelled by this creature I hadn't seen.

In the end, Mother settled the matter by saying, "Marriage is one's lot, appointed by heaven. Go to *Mawlana* and have him present Ameena to you. No one will compel you to marry her if you don't wish to. Make the prayer for guidance before you go, asking God to choose for you."

"If he stretches out his hand to me and says, 'I have given her to you in marriage,' what shall I say?"

"Tell him: 'There is no need to be in a hurry, *Mawlana*. Let me talk it over with my family first.'"

However, when I prayed in the Kaaba for guidance behind Ibrahim's shrine, I did not ask God to assist me in my choice, but rather to deliver me from Ameena.

The supper at *Mawland*'s house was the usual one of rich food, in contrast to our own supper at home, which consisted largely of cold dishes. The talk proceeded as always without any mention being made of Ameena or indeed of our previous conversation. When the meal was over and the servant had taken off the *mafatta*, in came Ameena carrying the tea tray with cups and pots, followed by the same servant with the rest of the tea things: the samovar and the small stand on which the utensils are laid.

"Peace be with you," she said, as she entered, in a clear, strong voice without any hint of shyness. Then she sat down and poured the tea into delicate cups and, having finished, returned the teapot to its place on the samovar. Having done this, she placed two cups on a small, silver-plated tray, stood up and moved toward us. As she approached *Mawlana*, she bent forward, placing her left hand on her breast, before extending the other hand to him, saying, "If you please, Father." She approached me in a similar fashion. Having returned to her place in the corner of the room, she too began to sip tea without appearing to pay any attention to what was going on. I glanced surreptitiously at her, taking care not to let her see me doing so, and once or twice I noticed she was endeavoring to get a glimpse of me in order to size me up. The impression I gained of her was not displeasing: though tall and plump, she had a cheerful face, with twinkling eyes and childlike, graceful movements that were without affectation.

Mawlana resumed the conversation he had begun at supper, relating one anecdote after another about this or that pious person, and the divine help they received in times of adversity. The virtuous people of whom he spoke were not just from the Muslims, but from other religions too. He possessed an abundant wealth of stories about the peoples before the Prophet's mission: those of Noah, Abraham and Moses.[48] Once only he raised his eyebrows and directed a question to Ameena about a book by al-Tanukhi,[49] possibly wanting to inform me by this that she was educated and well-read, or else he might simply have forgotten the title of the book and wished to avail himself of her youthful memory — it doesn't matter which.

Our soiree lasted longer than usual that evening. I was too embarrassed to ask permission to leave. I therefore stayed put, sitting cross-legged on the floor, or else squatting on my haunches, all the while cracking my knuckles to relieve the tension. It was I who was shy and not she, for I had the impression that I was the one being presented for approval. I found myself exceedingly embarrassed, while she retained a confident composure.

When she left, carrying the various tea things, I took leave of *Mawlana* without raising my eyes, and went away.

On the way home, I tried to organize my thoughts, for I anticipated the flood of questions which Mother would have ready for me. I lingered on my way, finding every excuse to divert my progress. Several times I asked myself, "What do you think, Muhaisin — yes or no?" As I couldn't find an answer, I hurried home. As I had expected, Mother was on her feet, and had evidently been pacing continuously around the house. She didn't even allow me a chance to catch my breath, but straightaway tilted my head back as though wishing to search my face to see the impression which that decisive meeting had left.

"What's the matter with you?" she asked. "You're pale—did things turn out badly?"

When I didn't reply, she repeated the question.

"Wait a little till I calm down," I said.

"Calm down from what? Is she beautiful? Did you like her?"

"I don't know."

"You don't know!" she exclaimed. "How is that?"

"I told you, I don't know."

"You're a strange fellow. Why don't you know? Tell me your impression of her. Is she fair-skinned and tall as her father told you?"

"Yes," I replied, "she is fair and tall."

"She pleased you then?"

"I didn't say so."

"What do you mean? If she is tall and fair, she must be beautiful."

"But Mother, it doesn't follow that every tall fair girl is beautiful."

"Then she must be ugly—does she have a bad complexion?"

"No, she has no visible defects."

"You're a strange fellow," she replied.

"Mother, believe me when I say that I can't formulate my feelings toward her. Perhaps I must see her again to define my feelings." Then I added, unconsciously: "Perhaps the matter isn't as simple as you imagine. It may be she who will decide, and not me."

"This is the first time I've ever heard such things spoken," she retorted. "It is the man who decides, not the woman! And what has she to decide? You have no flaws and any girl would be glad to have you for a husband."

"We'll see," I replied, turning toward the stairs in order to bring an end to the discussion. In the days preceding my next invitation to *Mawland*'s, I remained perplexed and uncertain as to what I should do. I tried to scrutinize his face to see if it offered enlightenment as to my situation. I wondered how I should proceed, and who should open the conversation, and what I would say to him should he ask the expected question. I began to think that, if considering marriage posed such difficult problems, then perhaps I should wait until I could make the required decision without so much distress. In time I was reminded of our next supper engagement, a date I had hardly forgotten. This time he searched my face with unaccustomed intensity, and spoke in a disjointed fashion foreign to him. I kept expecting him to extend his hand to me and say, "Will you accept Ameena as your wife?" And if I said "Yes," she would at once become my wife.

He might even ask me to take her home, since she would now be considered mine. I nearly cried out, imagining how the matter might be removed from my hands, so that I'd be married as it were by force. But why shouldn't I marry Ameena? What was wrong with her? The man had overwhelmed me with his generosity, opened his house to me and given me his daughter. Without warning, I heard him say in a deep voice, "Muhaisin, my son, there is a tradition which says that if someone comes along whose religiosity you approve of, then give him your daughter (or other female dependent) in marriage. I approve of your religiosity." After a brief pause, he continued, "Marriage is something that God ordains and not man, and while we may be willing, God does as He wills. If the matter were up to me alone, my decision would be immediate. However, Ameena has the right to choose or at least to consent to what I choose, and until now she hasn't given me her acquiescence." Having said that, he lapsed into silence.

Then, noticing that I was looking at him without really seeing him, he said: "Don't be sad. God may have someone more suitable in reserve for you. He may have decided that in order to fulfill His own purpose, Ameena is intended for someone else." Then, by way of consolation, he recited verses of poetry often quoted to assuage grief or sudden shock.

When I was able to regain control of my emotions, I said, "Do you mean that she refused to have me?"

"She didn't give her consent," he replied.

On the way home I lingered again, trying to come to terms with what had happened. I realized in those few minutes what a strange contradictory person lived inside me. I had fervently petitioned God to deliver me from her, but when He had done so, I expressed no thanks. Rather, I was overwhelmingly disappointed. Perhaps I felt disgraced and humiliated by her rejection of me, although I had been prepared to refuse her without considering her feelings or sense of humiliation and disappointment.

As always, Mother was waiting at the door to question me. "Well, did he suggest a date to solemnize the marriage by reciting the *Fatiha*?" she asked. "Did he fix the time of the marriage? I hope he is not thinking of having you live with them!"

I merely replied, "We agreed to postpone the matter until his daughter grows up a bit." I was unable to disclose even to my mother a situation in which I had been rejected, rather than serving as the authoritative party. Strangely enough, she said, "Maybe it's better that way." But why she said this, I don't know.

The whole subject moved from the area of consciousness to another realm, and was in time erased, for no other reason than that *Mawlana* proved himself to be a true man. He continued our special relationship as though nothing had happened, with invitations to supper, his usual reserved cheerfulness and inquiries after my mother. His disposition cheered me immensely, making me forget that I had been insulted in his own house, by the person nearest to him.

XXX

Without exception, all of the families in Mecca at this time undertook the pilgrimage year after year. They all had some involvement with the pilgrimage or the pilgrims, as agents, vendors or participants in the ceremony for its own sake. How easy it was at that time — all you had to do was to pray one prescribed prayer or another in the Holy Mosque, then go to al-Mudda'a, where you would find a file of cameleers and donkey drivers waiting for you, crying out "Ride for hire!" and advertising their conveyance. For a few piastres you would find yourself mounted on the back of one of them, alone or riding behind someone else if you so desired. You would thus be on your way to Arafa if you had delayed until the ninth day, or to Mina, if you were performing the pilgrimage of the Prophet.[50] On the ninth day of the pilgrimage there was scarcely a male to be found in Mecca, excepting the night watchmen and the *Khullaif*[51] thieves, as we called them. This band of thieves were insignificant in comparison with the pilgrimage thieves. The latter were notorious for sneaking into the pilgrims' tents on the evening of *Yaum al-Tarwiya*,[52] after everyone had retired for the night on the evening prior to reaching the Arafa station. From time to time you would hear intermittent cries of "Thieves, thieves!"—and then you would see the torchlit forms of the guides running in pursuit of their elusive suspects, without knowing who they were or where they had gone. The night would always be dark, that wonderful invention, electricity, not having been heard of yet, while torches and lanterns were confined to projecting over a limited radius.

On these particular nights, those who had stayed behind, largely the women who had elected not to undertake the pilgrimage that year for one reason or another, would gather together in an open space in the quarter, usually the Utaybiyya Quarter, to celebrate the Qays Festival until late at night. Crowds of women, unaccompanied by men, would be seen there shouting and chanting folksongs pertaining to this particular festival.

Although it is accepted that God has delivered us from this heresy, among others in the previous generation, nonetheless our women in the earlier part of the last century[53] were anxious to attend that festival in order to participate in the songs and to mitigate the loneliness of their staying behind in Mecca. As a child, it came about that on several occasions I had the opportunity to attend these Qays festivals. I helped carry the torches, walking in front of the women as they danced holding wooden swords in their hands. Although Mother never actually participated in the dance, she watched the festival, and carried a bag full of candied fruits and nuts, into which she repeatedly dipped her hand, and you could see her jaws moving constantly.

Although the last Qays Festival occurred a long time ago, the ambiguous nature of its ceremony left a permanent indelible impression on me. Various mythic elements were interwoven into this women's festival, all of them associated with how they had discovered a male intruder in their midst, wearing female clothes, carrying a sword, and convinced that his identity wouldn't be discovered. As always, the unpredictable happened, and the culprit was discovered and punished either by slapping or with the instrument of his wooden sword, and was further disgraced by the shame of his exposure in front of his family and relatives immediately after the feast. The matter invariably ended with the chief of the quarter heaping ridicule and rebuke on the offender and demanding that he solemnly swear that he would never commit such an aberration again.

Even before I had taken up the responsibilities of a teaching profession, the Qays celebration had long lost its appeal for me. The desire to participate in the activities of the pilgrimage assumed a strong affection. One opportunity open to me, and those like me, was to participate in guiding pilgrims at the Holy Mosque, as did dozens of boys of my age, either as helpers to the agents, or as single operators hunting down those without bedouin guides or those who wished to make additional circumambulations outside of the hours prescribed by the agents. This was a form of employment common to many of my generation. Participation in the *haj* festival in this way contributed toward our subsistence throughout the remaining months of the year. Even teachers took a part in it, offering their services to one of the agents. This category of teachers was regarded by people as being of a higher order than the free lancers who lay in wait at the many entrances to the Holy Mosque for pilgrims or those making the *umra*.

After examining most aspects of the tradition, I decided to adopt a different course, though one which was still connected with the pilgrimage and its celebration. I decided to work for the leading agent of our quarter as the secretary to his organization, bookkeeping, recording the names of the pilgrims, their steamship and the possessions they left in trust, as well as supervising the number of writs authorized for "substitutes," that is listing the names of those absent for whom the pilgrimage was to be made, the sums devoted to this purpose, and whether or not sacrificial animals were to be a part of the ceremony. We also kept a record of their general expenses, which included the rental of housing, camel litters, tents and camp sites at Mina, the meals provided for pilgrim guests, which were most often a banquet on the night of arrival from Jedda, and food supplied during the course of the pilgrimage, which included the farewell dinner after each group had made the final circumambulation in preparation for their departure.

The writs regarding "substitutes" formed an additional source of income, shrinking or expanding in accordance with the conscientiousness of the agent. The less honest would lock the money in their steel boxes without endeavoring to give any of it to anyone but themselves. Others would pick out some of the substitute documents for pilgrims, especially the richer ones—and from them give generously to themselves, their families and their top employees, distributing the rest to their servants, neighbors and some inhabitants of the quarter. Some of the writs would incur deficits less than the amounts designated, and thus contribute a profit to the agents. This was regarded as acceptable legal practice as long as the pilgrimage had been carried out in the name of the intended pilgrim who had not been able to perform the pilgrimage. If, for example, he or she had died and missed the opportunity of performing the pilgrimage, and therefore it devolved upon his or her relatives and heirs to either perform the pilgrimage for the deceased or else hire someone else to do so.

As it turned out, I didn't undertake the pilgrimage that year as a surrogate pilgrim, for this, according to the books of jurisprudence, is disallowed for one who has not performed the rite. This did not prevent me, however, from taking one of the documents in the name of my mother who, it had been decided, would make the pilgrimage in the agent's caravan. In my naivete, I decided to show one of these credit letters to the *Ustadh*, who, far from expressing interest, looked at me intently before saying in a dry, disinterested tone: "I do not make the pilgrimage for anyone else, nor have I any need to do so."

At the time I had not realized that those who accepted writs were generally simple folk with barely enough to live on, and not the sophists or the rich.

The day of ascent to Mina was an industrious one. The preparations made for it were not unlike those utilized for a military expedition, with the detailed regulations representing the accumulated experiences of over a thousand years. Preceding the caravan came the camels belonging to the "native Meccans," then the agent's family, who were mounted on four camels, then my own family. The camel litters, or *shagdufs*, of the "native Meccans" were distinguished from those of the other pilgrims in that the former were covered with smooth tugs, while the latter were covered with gunny sacking. The former sported brightly-colored railings in addition to having the fringes dyed red, while the other litters were of bare wood without the enhancement of any aesthetic detail. Even the camels chosen for the "native Meccans" seemed to be larger and of a more dignified bearing than those of the other pilgrims.

Once the *shagdufs* had been fastened to the camels, the latter were arranged in a long column, with the camel drivers strategically distributed so that the halter of the leading camel was taken by the oldest and most experienced cameleer. The other drivers were spread out along both sides of the caravan, each of them responsible for several camels, while two walked at the rear. Since the caravan was made up of Egyptian pilgrims, their native ululations were heard as soon as the leading camel was set in motion, to be followed by singing and chanting until we had left the houses of Mecca behind, heading eastward on the road to *al-masha'ir*, or the holy places outside of Mecca.

The practical reason for the strategic distribution of camel drivers was the fear that an assailant might have the temerity, when the congestion increased, to split off a portion of the caravan by detaching the guide-rope, thus separating the rear of the caravan from the front. The rear section could thus become lost for hours or possibly days without anyone knowing its fate. This was a common occurrence, unless an experienced person noticed quickly and set up a cry: "Brigands, O camel drivers, brigands!" This would then lead to the reunion of the separated halves.

Those of us who operated as employees of an agent, whom we called *"Amm,"* equipped ourselves with a bedouin bag, in place of the elegant attache cases carried by businessmen today, and a belt worn over the gown. We also carried a curved cudgel, given to us by our employer, with which to defend ourselves in case of emergency.

Although I walked most of the way to Mina and Arafa, I was so intoxicated by the mission that I was oblivious of the fatigue induced by walking so far. I persisted in walking despite Mother's calling out from time to time: "Get up onto the *shagduf*, son, and have a rest. Are you a camel driver?" But I resisted her entreaty as I enjoyed walking with the cameleers and the servants. I asked the head camel driver how many times he had made the pilgrimage and about his experiences. He had a lively memory, rich with accounts of the terrors that he and the pilgrims had endured either on the pilgrimage to Mecca or when visiting Medina.

One of the most disturbing things he related was the phenomenon of those camel drivers who used to conspire with the brigands against the pilgrims instead of rightfully defending them. He told me of how he had lost a son during a raid in which the visiting pilgrims resisted with force instead of surrendering. They fought the raiders at one of the stations on the road to Medina, using staves, stones and whatever came to hand, with the result that the thieves were defeated, leaving two dead, one of them his son. After this the camel driver reformed his ways and began to defend his caravan if need be, instead of handing it over to the hungry Bedouin and marauding cutthroats. He had an extraordinary ability to talk incessantly, as though his narrations were a prerecorded tape, or as though he were reading from the written page. His stories followed on without any interruption, and, judging by the avidity with which he chattered, it was clear that he rarely found so receptive an ear.

At intervals, he would take off toward the rear to check on his camels and their riders, issuing instructions to his team of drivers to watch a certain camel because it was unreliable or to treat another gently because it was ailing. He kept a constant count of the camels, and only when satisfied that everything was proceeding as it should, would he return to the head of the caravan, and resume talking where he had left off. He would invariably begin his stories with the same sentence: "Once when we were on a visit to Medina," or "One time we were on a pilgrimage," and proceed from there. If I had possessed the facilities at the time, I would have recorded all of his stories and published them. They were a remarkable mixture of the comic and terrifying, and included a great deal of information about camels, the maladies to which they were susceptible, their life span, the stations on this or that route which provided water and those that provided none, incidents of death by thirst, the constant fighting between al-Safra' and al-Furaish tribes along the way to Medina, the tribes most notorious for raiding the caravans, and the most illustrious and courageous cameleers of his day.

During the narration of these stories, one or more wayside beggars would appear, armed with a long stick, to the end of which was nailed an empty tomato-paste can which rattled. This he would raise in front of one of the litters, calling out, "O pilgrims, may God accept your pilgrimage."[54] From time to time one would hear the clatter of a coin as it struck the brandished can. Upon this the beggar would move on to the next camel and the next...

Mother was determined to treat me as a juvenile on the occasion of the big feast day at the end of the pilgrimage. Collecting together a number of small children from the encampment, she produced a bag of candied fruits and nuts which she threw over me, and laughingly sang out: "They went on a pilgrimage and came back." The children grabbed the scattered pieces, while the agent and his family laughed and shouted at this singular sight. The game ended with her draping a *qilada* round my neck, resembling a necklace and composed of dried dates sold during the pilgrimage season for this very purpose. They are sold also before the sacred al-Fitr[55] Feast at the end of Ramadan for the making of *dibyaza*. It seems unnecessary for me to relate here how this substance is formed, for most of the Meccan families and some of those in Jedda are still expert in its composition, despite its unpopularity with the present generation.

The nights spent at Mina were truly happy ones, full of jubilation, in which we strolled about the Arab bazaar, observing the itinerants and the women "who had not made the pilgrimage simply from a desire to obtain merit with God." The atmosphere exalted one, as did the various evening celebrations, such as gathering round a Qur'anic reciter seated on an agent's bench, or around a group of Arab tribesmen chanting and dancing as though at a wedding. All of this was an important part of the sights of Mina.

XXXI

In the stories that Mother used to tell me as a child, the hero, whether al-Shatir Hasan[56] or someone else, was always born on the night on which the story was begun. On the second night, he would meet his "princess" or the girl of his dreams, snatch her up and bear her off on horseback to live with her on some cloud or other, or within the walls of an enchanted castle. On the third night, the destroyer of pleasure and the severer of ties would suddenly fall upon them. This was the natural chain of events, unless Mother was not in the mood for stories, in which event the hero would be born, marry or not marry, and die all in one night. It was the events of the second night that I most anticipated, in which the hero undertook amazing adventures and fought tremendous battles for the love of the girl of his dreams, or, if it happened that it was she who was in pursuit of him, then enchantresses and witches would be used to secure the girl's ends. Since the activities of birth, marriage and death all took place within a space of three nights, the impression left deep inside one, was that "story children" grew up quickly and died quickly. It never occurred to me then, that life resembled fiction. Suddenly the hero — and each of us is that to himself, God be praised — finds himself arrived at the second night, or at the third, in the flash of an eye. Otherwise, how should I interpret my sudden realization that the principal of the school had grown old and retired, and with old age had come an end to those pleasures common to youth, and finally death itself. I sat on his tomb, reciting "If the two angels come to you, etc." And how else could I account for the rapid succession of events in my own life, my long affiliation with the school as a teacher, then as a supervisor, then as assistant to the principal? And Jameela too had grown up in front of my eyes and was now a mature woman, who diffused her femininity whenever she came to class. These lessons had continued for so long that I could scarcely find a subject or book to teach her, for she devoured knowledge with the insatiable appetite of one of the grasshoppers that periodically attacked the gardens of Ta'if, leaving nothing but dry stalks.

How could all this have happened without my being aware of the tremendous speed with which time passes? No doubt this is one of the impenetrable riddles of existence which decrees the annihilation of every generation in the space of fifty years, which was the average life span in those days, and their replacement by new children of the earth who ensure the rejuvenation of life and the perpetuation of its marvelous cycle.

I was over thirty years old when I discovered this, I think — for my birthday remains an enigma, neither registered in any book nor recollected exactly by anyone. This realization came to me in Ta'if,[57] where it had become a habit with us to go each year along with the elite of Quraish[58] and Mecca, something they had, in fact, done ever since the discovery of this ready-made summer resort.

That night I returned to our house couched on top of the eminence known as Bab al-Rai'. I noticed nothing unusual until suppertime, when Mother didn't sit down with me as usual, but excused herself saying that she had no appetite. When I pressed her, she did sit down and begin to eat, but without relish, taking a sip of water between every bite. When she had finished, she folded up the *mafatta* on which the food had been laid out, and retired without saying anything. In the course of the next few days, I grew alarmed at her loss of appetite. Without being able to discern what was wrong, I noticed that she never swallowed a morsel without taking a mouthful of water. She didn't complain but was wasting away. When the summer had nearly come to an end, we returned to Mecca without waiting for the season known as the "rosy period," which comes between the close of the summer and the beginning of fall, when the resort is at its most beautiful. That is the time when the first sting of cold enters the atmosphere, adding a red tinge to the faces of those on vacation. Others find their skin begins to chafe and peel around the edges of their lips and cheeks, a sure indication that it is time to depart and leave the resort to its permanent residents who are resilient to the dry cold. No, this time we didn't wait for the "rosy period," nor did we take back with us sacks of pomegranates, grapes and quinces to relatives and friends who had been unable to summer with the more fortunate ones.

Once at Mecca, we began to look at the matter in another light. It was now clear to me that Mother was ill. To me, this was a strange phenomenon, as I had never known her to be indisposed in this fashion before. She had, of course, suffered from occasional colds, which she treated herself with certain herbs drawn from the dozens which filled a small medicine case. She used to get headaches, which were easily cured by inhaling from a bottle of sal ammoniac which she kept ready at hand. Likewise, she had her own applications of *karabash* for stomach ache and pains in the side, sometimes applying a poultice on the sensitive area. All of that was done as a matter of course without anyone taking particular notice. It was quite normal to see her adopting the Meccan custom of wearing a headband for the remedy of headaches.

But this time there was no relatable precedent to her illness. I had never prepared myself for the possibility of her being ill, and was at a loss how to act. It seemed the first thing to do was to enlist the advice of our neighborhood women, including that of *Amm* Umar's wife. Numerous opinions were proposed, and Mother consented to the one which seemed most applicable to her symptoms, namely her difficulty in swallowing food and the resultant discomfort that must have come from an evil eye unsanctioned by the Prophet, that is, one belonging to an envious person who had resented her eating and shot an arrow at her. The morsel of food which had been hit had thus stuck in her throat, and denied the descent of further food. The only chance for a cure was to consult so-and-so, who was in al-Ma'abida, and who was famous for his skill in extracting morsels from constricted throats. I consented to the proposition, and that same afternoon Mother, our female neighbor and I were conveyed to al-Ma'abida by horse and carriage, the two of them seated inside the carriage, while I sat beside the driver. The man's expertise was sufficient to extract the offending morsel of food, which he showed to us on an offensively odorous wad of wet cotton.

"This is the particle of *ma'sub*," he said, "which a hungry envious person looked at and coveted, so that it stuck in her throat." I tried to recall the possible culprit. Unable to cast any light on the matter, I ventured the solution that it could have been someone who saw me buying *ma'sub* from Barhat al-Qazzaz one day, and loosed his arrow, hitting that delicacy, so that when Mother ate it, she was stricken. I take refuge with the Lord "from the evil of the envious when he envies."[59]

Contrary to expectation, Mother did not recover with the extraction of the congesting morsel of food. It's true that for a day or two our hopes were raised, and we imagined that she had begun to eat and swallow without having to assist the operation by the intake of water. We assumed that her reliance on water as a dissolvant had lessened, and would continue to do so gradually until she returned to normal. When she failed to recover, we again had recourse to the wise women of our quarter. They offered a series of suggestions, and prescribed herbs to be steeped, or powdered and swallowed dry, or formed into small paste balls which appeared quite disproportionate in size to the restrictive size of the throat. Mother endured it all patiently, swallowing the dry powders in the morning, and the balls of paste in the evening, persisting in these remedies despite the fact she nearly choked. After a period of three weeks, the balls seemed to bring about some temporary relief, and for a while she could take food somewhat more easily than before.

But this was immediately followed by a relapse, during which the passage of her throat became so restricted that it prevented the intake of any food. She could no longer contemplate solid foods, and had to turn for sustenance to soups, imbibing *al-hareera* and, in the morning, a little milk from our goat, "*Umm* al-Khair."

After a time, we again took up the search for a cure, and experimented with *al-mahw*—a remedy prepared by al-Sayyid so-and-so. *Al-mahw* consists of the writing of Qur'anic verses on earthenware bowls, into which the patient pours water carried from the Zamzam Well, in which the verses written in China ink are dissolved. The bitter-tasting infusion with its unpalatable acidity is then drunk by the patient. Mother drank dozens of bowls of this daily, but to little effect.

Following the failure of this remedy, the *Sayyid* decided to seclude her, and set up a white curtain around her couch, so that she was cut off from human company for seven days. This proving to be of no avail, they hung a charm around her neck, and brought in a professional Shangeeti *shaikh*[60] to read the Ya Sin *sura* around her bed for a number of days. I conceded to any suggestion, reasonable or unreasonable. I'm ashamed to recollect the nature of some of the experiments performed on her — may God have mercy on her — which met with my approval, blindly bent on seeing her cured.

After several months of experimentation, I finally considered calling in a doctor from the only hospital I knew of in Mecca, called the Takirya. The doctor agreed to visit only after he was assured that I had a whole riyal with which to pay him for his professional services. I carried his medical bag while he followed behind with quick steps. The examination took no more than a few minutes, after which the doctor diagnosed cancer of the larynx and possibly the esophagus too. As this was the first time I had heard of the disease called cancer, I was at a loss as to how to interpret his diagnosis. When I asked the doctor what we could do, he replied that the cancer was at an advanced stage and her general condition very poor. Nevertheless, he wrote a prescription and told me to give it to her. After I had secured the medicine from the hospital pharmacy, as was customary in those days, I returned to her, perplexed and more pessimistic than before. When she had taken the medicine for a few days, but without any apparent benefit, I went back to the doctor, but he refused to visit Mother saying: "I don't wish to take advantage of your money. Your mother's case is hopeless. She will live out her appointed time, and then leave this world. We are all going the same way, so don't be unduly distressed, and be a man."

Throughout this distressing period, *Amm* Umar's family lent me every support. My main meal of the day, luncheon, came from their house, carried by their own servant or by Jameela herself in a multi-tiered lunch container. And *Amm* Umar's wife spent most of the morning at our house, keeping Mother company. She would return home at noon to prepare the food, leaving Jameela behind until I came back from school. Jameela would then return home as part of the rotatory system, so that the lunch bearer could undertake his task, and so on.

My attachment to them grew with each day. *Amm* Umar's solicitude and general sympathy calmed my spirit when I visited him in the afternoons. As usual, he spoke little other than to repeat the *hawqala* formula. His silence would deepen whenever I related the various methods of treatment and magic which were tried out on Mother in pursuit of a cure. But when he learned that she had cancer, of which I knew nothing, he increased his oral ritual, and looked suddenly despondent.

Some days later, he spoke of a new medicine called "penicillin" which had been discovered during the First World War. While it remained in short supply, it was known that a doctor in one of the Jedda consulates possessed a small quantity of it. Complications arose from the doctor's being a Christian, and therefore prohibited entry into Mecca, while

Mother could not be taken to Jedda. It was decided therefore that *Amm* Umar would bring the penicillin himself and leave it with the doctor at the Takiyya Hospital who would inject her every few hours. All would be agreed upon if only I gave my consent. I mulled it over in my unconscious — a Christian doctor . . . a consulate . . . and the wonderful discovery of penicillin. Why not? We had tried everything else, even cauterization, which made her sides and chest bleed. So be it; we had nothing to lose by experimentation.

This penicillin worked almost immediately, and after a few days, her condition improved. She was able to sit up on the couch for the first time since her illness, and take the soup in her trembling hand in a manner that had us believe she was cured. But this was far from the true nature of things, for, after a brief respite, she had an even more violent relapse than before. It was evident that she was in excruciating pain, which had her give constant voice to her suffering. For several nights she hardly slept, while I squatted beside her, convincing myself that my staying awake was a vital key to her survival.

One morning she closed her eyes in my presence, never to open them again.

XXXII

After the mourners had departed, I sat down on the moist tomb scarcely able to believe that the person closest to me now lay beneath the stones which the grave-digger had packed into the earth. I was numb, I could neither think nor feel pain; I wasn't even conscious of what was or wasn't going on around me. I sat there until I recovered my senses, and remembered the *sura* of Ya Sin, which I continued to recite until my throat grew dry and darkness had fallen

Finally, the cemetery guard reminded me that it was illegal for me to remain there any longer. I stood up, dazed, and proceeded toward the main entrance. After making my exit from the cemetery, I stood in front of Sayyid's coffeehouse, not knowing where to go. Just as one presses a computer key, causing lights to show up on the screen, so various places flashed to mind. The coffeehouse in the Jinn's Haunt, the Holy Mosque, home, my childhood school, innumerable places, some of which it was implausible to visit, some of which no longer existed, and some of which

I had not seen for many years. None of them seemed a wise option, so I abandoned myself to instinctive wandering. I found myself returning the way we had come, carrying the coffin, and passed the place where the *Fatiha* had been recited, and on to al-Mudda'a, and al-Mas'a, turning aside into al-Safa Rise, then to Saqifat al-Safa, which people usually avoided after nightfall. But unconscious of the night or darkness, I continued on my way. Entering the Saqifa left me with the strange sensation that I was regressing to my mother's womb. How, I wondered, can a man experience so profound and unshareable an emotion. When a flicker of light appeared at the end of the covered Saqifa, I almost faltered, but decided to go on.

It occurred to me after a time that my appearance was attracting the attention of passersby, for whenever I came near a lamp post or light of any sort, I noticed that people looked at me in the same way, staring first at my head and then at my feet. I assumed that I must have lost my shoes and my turban, but how could a man lose his shoes when he was wearing them? They must have come off, I thought, together with my turban, when I went down into that dark hole to lay Mother's dear face in the dust — this was the only explanation. More than one person whom I met must have tried to console me, either by taking my hand or embracing me. This must have happened, or else I dreamed it one night after that night of terror. I still remember words that were spoken, and how can a person remember something that was never said to him?

As soon as I arrived home, I went straight to her couch. Why not? Shouldn't a man reassure himself about his sick mother before going to sleep? But what was that light at the far end of the room, and who were those people sitting waiting? It was *Amm* Umar and his whole family. When I had assured myself it was they, he came and took me in his arms, crying as he did so. But why? Then it was his wife who began to kiss my head and both my cheeks—quite unaccountably. Then I remembered that it had been said to me once that he was a Freemason, and that it had been rumored in the quarter that he was a spy for the British. For a moment I had the strange feeling that their intention was to form a circle around me and push me gently out of the door and into the street, and then it was actually happening; but why? And without them so much as uttering a word, and without me saying anything either, I was floating in the space between the house and the street. Was I floating, or did someone carry me — how was I to know?

XXXIII

I discovered for the first time that one could hold a cup of tea while sitting asleep on a latticed balcony. I awoke to find myself in this situation. Had I really been asleep or had I lost the power of sight which suddenly returned to me? Upon this abrupt awakening, I was surprised to hear a voice ring out in a sharp cry, "O Mother." *Amm* Umar trembled violently on hearing my exclamation, while his wife hastened to pull me to her breast, stroking me as she invoked the name of God and uttered the *hawqala* formula. Without knowing why I continued to repeat my cry. After a few moments I heard *Amm* Umar say: "He is getting his memory back. Let him cry and scream — his consciousness is coming to terms with what has happened. He is on the road to recovery."

Who was this person on the road to recovery?

During another of my conscious periods he said to me — or was he lying? — "You were in a state of total collapse. For two weeks you have persisted in this state, but, thank God, you are better now."

XXXIV

I didn't return home or see that couch again. Nor do I know what happened to the tall lamp in the corner of the room or who milked "*Umm al-Khair*," or whether the rabbits still lived in their customary burrows. The one thing that was clear was that someone had brought my clothes to *Amm* Umar's place where I now lived, something confirmed by the fact that I wore my habitual clothes.

Though I didn't return home, I went back to my teaching post. *Amm* Umar convinced me to do so. "You cannot absent yourself any longer," he said. "The principal has asked about you on several occasions, and most of the staff have visited you a number of times; but of course I took the precaution that no one should see you until you had recovered your health. You need to get outside of these four walls and meet people."

Taking heed of his advice, I returned to school and generally enjoyed my duties, in spite of the fact that I would walk around in the school like a sleep walker. If I had been asked to write a paper at that time describing my feelings, I would have returned a blank answer sheet. Nevertheless, I taught, discussed things with the students and corrected their notebooks. My duties fulfilled, I retreated into an inaccessible psychological seclusion, taking refuge in silence. No one harassed me by attempting to intrude on my feelings: I just discharged my duties and then left.

I must have spent a long time at *Amm* Umar's house, though I still don't remember going to it on the night I was ejected from the cemetery. However, I continued to occupy the room put aside for me beside the library, and this seemed proof enough of my living there. The afternoon ritual of sipping tea behind the latticed balcony provided further evidence of my having come to this house by some means or other to live with its inhabitants. I didn't ask myself how long I would stay there, whether my presence was a burden to the family, or, if I left them, where I would go. I didn't raise any of these questions and no one alluded to them. It seemed perfectly natural to be there—and, as far as I knew, no one raised any objections. On the contrary, I was made unconditionally welcome, although there was something peculiar in the situation and in my conversation with the family and with *Amm* Umar. The rule, whenever he and I met, was to speak just to the point; he didn't say much, nor did I.

Then, one afternoon — it must have been months later — as we were sitting together as usual, he appeared to be preparing himself to announce something out of the ordinary. "Muhaisin," he said, after some hesitation, "It seems to me you need someone to keep you company and divert your thoughts from their lonely preoccupation," and then he stopped.

After an interval he added, "Nothing relieves one's inner loneliness better than a good wife with whom one can feel at home," and, having said this, he again lapsed into silence.

It was clear that it was costing him a lot of effort to come to the point of his speech. Then he suddenly changed his usual manner of conversing to ask, "Have you never thought of getting married?"

"I did once."

"Then you are not against the idea of marriage itself?"

"I am not a sworn enemy of it."

"In that case" he said, "I am offering you my daughter Jameela in marriage. Would you accept her?"

Having raised the question that had clearly been burdening him, he took a deep breath. As for me, I was once again seeing that screen with its dancing points of light which I had first known on the night of the burial, and with its dark paint full of words, places and names with no connecting threads, at which I continued to stare.

When I failed to answer, he said: "What did you say?"

"I didn't say anything."

"Don't you want to say anything?"

"But the second night always came before the third," I replied without thinking.

He rubbed his forehead like one occupied in deep thought, intent on deciphering the meaning of what I had said. After a while he remarked, appearing to have figured out my meaning: "Life generally goes along on one plane, but it doesn't do so in all matters. Life and death follow each other, but no one knows which was the first—night or day."

I was unable to reply as the lights were flashing on the screen, so each of us went his own way.

XXXV

"The best names are surely Muhammad or 'Umar, or their derivatives [61]," he said to me by way of opening his conversation. Since his distortion of the tradition was evident, as were his intentions, namely that I should call my son after him, I answered: "I want to call my son Muhaisin Muhaisin."

"Do you want to call him Muhaisin so his name will be Muhaisin, son of Muhaisin?" he inquired.

"No, I want to call him Muhaisin Muhaisin. Do you remember the first story I read in your library?" I asked.

"Yes."

"The title was "John III," I said.

"I remember."

"Do you recall that when I asked you its meaning, you told me that the hero's name was John, as was his father's and grandfather's, which is the reason they wrote his name as John III?"

"I remember."

"I am not sure that my son Muhaisin will likewise name his son Muhaisin," I added. "Therefore I shall name him Muhaisin Muhaisin, so that he will be forced to write in Muhaisin Muhaisin, son of Muhaisin."

Turning away, he whispered in a voice which he thought I would not hear—I swear to that—"There are many kinds of madness."

ENDNOTES

[1] *'Arafa* Day: The ninth day of the annual pilgrimage to Mecca. 'Arafa is a hill some twenty-one kilometers east of Mecca, where some of the central rites of the pilgrimage are performed.

[2] *Ba* and *ta* : Two consecutive letters in the Arabic alphabet written in a similar way, differing only in the dots above or below the letters.

[3] *Rasheeda Reader:* An elementary reader for beginners.

[4] There is a proverb in Arabic which says, "The best names are those derived from 'Abd or Muhammad." 'Abd means the worshipper of God, and Muhammad is the Prophet's name. There are numerous names beginning with 'Abd, such as 'Abd al-Khaliq (Worshipper of the Creator), 'Abd al-Rahman (Worshipper of the Merciful), etc. From Muhammad many proper nouns are derived such as Ahmad, Hamid, Hameed, Hammad, Hamad, etc.

[5] *Al-Duhul* : Meaning simpleton, fool.

[6] The Year of the Elephant: An elephant was given as a gift by some Indian dignitaries to the Sherif of Mecca, 'Awn al-Rafiq Pasha ibn Muhammad (ruled Mecca 1299—1323 A.H./1882-1905 A.D.), who seems to have been a tyrant. The elephant remained in Mecca several years and caused a great amount of destruction. It lived on the property of the Sherif's palace and was taken out twice a week by its special servant to be washed. The servant would pass with it through the main street of town, with grocery shops on each side selling bread, vegetables, and dairy products. The elephant would stretch its trunk and take whatever it wanted from these shops without their owners daring to prevent it or pushing it off. This continued until an unknown person lay in wait for it one day and shot it with a bullet. This took place two years before the death of the Sherif. Bogary must have been alluding to this incident as the 'Year of the Elephant'.

[7] The Year of the Big Flood : This is the big flood which surprised Mecca in 1360 A.H. (1941 A.D.). It assailed the Kaaba and carried off all that it found on its way, causing much havoc and disarray.

[8] The Year of Mercy : In 1310 A.H. (1892 A.D.) a cholera epidemic in Mecca killed thousands of people. It happened during the pilgrimage season, and thousands of pilgrims had to interrupt their

pilgrimage and return to their country. The word "mercy" might have been used out of belief that people who die while performing the *hajj* are engulfed by God's mercy.

9 This is a reference to the Quranic story of Joseph, son of Jacob, who was put in prison at the instigation of the Pharaoh's wife, whose seduction he had resisted. According to the Quranic story, Joseph had two companions in prison, each of whom had a dream which Joseph interpreted. The first dreamed that he was pressing wine, and the second that he carried bread on his head at which birds were picking. Joseph explained that the first would become cup bearer to the Pharaoh and the second would be crucified and birds would pick at his head.

10 This refers to the fourteenth century *Hijri* (or A.H.) of the Islamic calendar. The beginning of the fifteenth century A.H., on *Muharram* first, coincides with 21 November 1979. The Muslims date their calendar from the year the Prophet emigrated (*hajara*, hence *hijri*) from Mecca to Medina to escape the persecution of his own tribe of Quraish, whose age-old supremacy over the Meccans and the Kaaba and their superiority among the Arabs were threatened by the rising tide of Islam. The first *Hijri* year coincides with 622 A.D. It should be added here that the Islamic calender is a lunar, not a solar, calender. This means that a *Hijri* year is about eleven days shorter than a Gregorian year.

11 The period of one hundred days is required to determine whether a woman had become pregnant by her now-deceased husband.

12 Badr: The name of a small town south west of Medina at the junction of a road from Mecca to Syria. Here a great battle took place between the Prophet's followers and his tribe of Quraish. The battle was won by the Muslims who were far outnumbered by the Qurashites. The latter lost many of their most eminent men, suffering a catastrophic defeat. This took place in the second year of the Islamic Calendar (624 A.D.).

13 Dhu al-Rumma : (77-117 A.H./696-735 A.D.) One of the greatest of the Umayyad poets who wrote much fine poetry about the desert, describing it minutely.

14 Al-Furaish : A village between Mecca and Medina famous for the parsimoniousness of its people.

15 Quranic verse, *sura* 7, verse 176.

16 A famous verse in Arabic with which the poet 'Ali ibn al-Jahm addressed al-Mutawakkil, the Caliph of Baghdad: "You are like the dog in your loyalty, and like a billy goat in your endurance against calamities." The

verse was regarded by the Caliph as a non-urban way of address.

[17] A tradition of the Phrophet, which says, "If a dog should lick out of a plate, then wash it seven times, one of which is to be with earth."

[18] *Al-Haballo* and *Hammar.* As in other cultures, Arabs nickname people by their negative qualities or by their professions, even when these are menial. *Al-Haballo* means "the stupid one," and *Hammar* means "donkey driver."

[19] Portraiture and statuary were forbidden in Islam for fear of idolatry.

[20] *Shangeeti* refers to a resident of the city of Shangeet in Mauritania in West Africa. This town has produced many learned men well versed in Islamic studies and Quranic recitals. Several families bearing the name "Shangeeti" live now as citizens of various Arab countries. However, as is revealed later in the novel, the word "Shangeeti" would mean a man knowledgeable in the art of magic and charms, as many people who came from Shangeet took to this occult profession as they traversed the Arab world eastward.

[21] Abu Righal: According to popular Islamic belief, Abu Righal was a man from the tribe of Thaqif who is said to have led Abraha, the South Arabian king, on his way to Mecca during the famous war (mentioned in the Quran) launched by Abraha on the holy city in the sixth century. It is believed that the raid took place in the same year in which the Prophet was born (570 A.D.). The attack was a failure. Abu Righal was buried in al-Mughammas and it has been a custom to stone his tomb.

[22] Most Arabic words are vowelized at the end, changing their vowels according to their function in the sentence.

[23] Ibn Malik and his Alfiyya: Ibn Malik is Abu 'Abdallah Jamal al-Din al-Ta'i (601-672 A.H./1203-1274 A.D.). He was an Andalusian by origin but emigrated to Syria. He was a great philologist and wrote many books and treatises. His most famous work is his *Alfiyya*, a comprehensive treatise of a thousand verses (hence *alfiyya*, "a thousander") versifying Arabic grammar for students to memorize.

[24] Sunni (as opposed to Shi'a) Muslims have four sects: Hanafi, Shafi'i, Maliki, and Hanbali. Some Muslim countries have a predominance of one sect, e.g. most Turks are Hanafis, and most North Africans are Malikis.

[25] All descendants of the Prophet are the children of his daughter, Fatima, and 'Ali ibn Abi Talib, the Prophet's cousin. They are regarded as dignitaries. The prophet had no surviving sons.

[26] A tradition of the Prophet says "The services due from one Muslim to another are

six: If you meet him, greet him; if he invites you, accept his invitation; if he asks your advice, give him advice; if he sneezes and thanks God, tell him "God bless you"; if he falls sick, visit him; and if he dies, walk in his funeral."

[27] The Ya Sin *sura* is regarded as a special sura and is recited on important occasions for grace. It is number 36 of the Quran.

[28] *Sura* Ya Sin, verse 83.

[29] *Sura* 31, verse 34.

[30] These were the two major schools of Arabic grammar in medieval times.

[31] *Jabart:* or *Jabarti:* A name given to Muslims coming from Ethiopia either to study Islamic sciences (there is a position in al-Azhar Mosque in Cairo named after them), or to be near the holy places. A *rabat* here means a kind of hostel for special nationalities. Such hostels existed in Mecca. *Rabat* here should not be confused with the military *rabat* used in other historical texts to mean a garrison post.

[32] *al-Milal wa 'l-Nihal* is a famous treatise on religions and sects written by Muhammad b. 'Abd al-Karim al-Shahrastani (d. 1153 A.D.). The treatise is regarded as one of the remarkable documents on the philosophical literature of the Arabs. The author reviews all the philosophical and religious systems that he was able to study and classes them according to their degree of remoteness from Muslim theology.

[33] These are two dissimilar Islamic sects; the Rafidites were a Shi'a sect of the eighth century, and the Jahmiyyas were an early theological sect which contradicted orthodox beliefs regarding some of the attributes of God.

[34] Al-Sumaw'al: This is al-Sumaw'al ibn 'Adiya', said to be a Jewish-Arab poet whose residence was in the strong castle of al-Ablaq near Taima' in northern Arabia. He is renowned for loyalty to his pledge, and the proverb "more loyal than al-Sumaw'al" has come down through the centuries. He lived in the middle of the sixth century A.D.

[35] Al-Mutanabbi: (915-955 A.D.) One of the most famous poets of the Arabic language. Dabba was a man from Iraq known for his treachery and stinginess. When al-Mutanabbi, on a trip with a group of noblemen from Kufa, stopped at Dabba's place, he refused to give them hospitality. The noblemen asked al-Mutanabbi to satirize him, which the poet did reluctantly. It is said that it was this Dabba who, with a group of thugs, set out to ambush al-Mutanabbi in an uneven battle which ended with the death of al-Mutanabbi and his son.

[36] The *Mahjar* Poets: *Mahjar* means place of emigration, and these were the

émigré Arab poets to America who rose to fame during the first four decades of the twentieth century. Among them are Gibran Kahlil Gibran and Ilya Abu Madi.

[37] There is a clear distinction in most cases in Arabic between the feminine and the masculine genders, which is marked usually (but not exclusively) by differences in word endings, whether verbs or nouns.

[38] He is speaking here of the Islamic calendar (see note 9).

[39] Quranic verse, *sura* 39, verse 9.

[40] Zamzam well : The famous well near the Kaaba in Mecca from which all pilgrims drink. It is customary in some Arab countries to wish a person to "drink from Zamzam, God willing," i.e. to be able to fulfill the deep wish of every pious Muslim to perform the holy pilgrimage.

[41] It is a testimony to the unity of Arabic culture that the habit of offering parts of a cooked lamb to someone with the purpose of symbolizing something is found in various Arab countries. Here the offering of the larger part of the sheep's tongue is meant as a mock suggestion that *Mawlana*, to whom the tongue was offered, was either not very eloquent or too talkative. Of course, this was meant only as a joke in this context.

[42] Shaaban: The Hijri month preceding Ramadan, the month of fasting.

[43] The '*Amma* part of the Quran is the first part taught to beginners.

[44] Majnun Layla, or Qais ibn al-Mulawwah, was a famous love poet of the Umayyad period (the seventh-eighth centuries). His real identity has never been ascertained, but he became a central figure for love literature in Arabic. Layla was his beloved cousin whom he was not allowed to marry, a situation which caused him to become demented. His *diwan*, or collection of poetry, contains beautiful lyrical poems extolling the value of love and its undying qualities.

[45] This alludes to a piece of modern verse by Ahmad Shawqi (1869-1932): "A look, then a smile, then a greeting, then a conversation, then a rendezvous agreement, then a meeting."

[46] It is customary that the *imams* (religious leaders) leading the prayers on Fridays in the greater mosques of Islam recite the *sura* of *Sajda* (*sura* 32) during the first phase of the dawn prayer. The *sura*'s theme is the mystery of creation, the mystery of time, and the mystery of man's final end. The contemplation of these mysteries should lead to faith and the worship of the Creator.

[47] Night-time prayers, or *al-tahajjud*, are prayers over and above the

obligatory prayers that are made five times a day (at dawn, noon, afternoon, sunset and evening). Night prayers are made by the very pious who stay up at night or wake up before dawn for worship.

48 Muslims respect both Christianity and Judaism and believe in their prophets. However, Muslims have certain reservations about some of their beliefs.

49 Al-Tanukhi: Abu 'Ali al-Muhassin, a jurist and writer of the tenth century A.D.

50 A description of the pilgrimage rites during the last days of the *hajj* is necessary here. On the eighth day of the month of Dhu al-Hijja, the month of the *Hajj*, many (but not necessarily all) pilgrims go to Mina, one of three holy places of the pilgrimage outside Mecca called al-Masha'ir. Mina is situated east of Mecca on the road to 'Arafa. Muslims must spend day nine of Dhu al-Hijja in 'Arafa and those who do not go to Mina on the eighth day, go straight to 'Arafa, arriving there that evening. The pilgrims leave 'Arafa the evening of the ninth day and go to al-Muzdalifa, situated between 'Arafa and Mina. At dawn on day ten, the pilgrims leave for Mina to celebrate the Feast of al-Adha (Sacrifice) where the sacrifice of animals and the clipping of hair and nails take place. The morning of the al-Adha feast, they throw stones on Jamrat al-'Aqaba or the great *jamra* in Mina, symbolizing the throwing of stones on the devil. Pilgrims who stay to celebrate the rest of the days (the eleventh, twelvth and thirteenth) at Mina will cast each day seven stones at each of the three *jamras* (i.e. the three columns of stones surrounded by troughs into which the stones fall): the great *jamra* further to the right as the road leaves Mina and climbs toward the mountains in the direction of Mecca, the middle *jamra* and the first *jamra*, these last two being some 150 meters apart. The days at Mina after the return from 'Arafa are days of great jubilation and illumination. The pilgrimage of the Prophet is the one that goes on the eighth day of Dhu 'l-Hijja to Mina, then to 'Arafa.

51 These are the thieves who stay behind when the city is almost emptied of most of its men who go on the Pilgrimage. *Khullaif* means "stay behind." Others who stay behind are those who have a good reason to do so, mostly women and children. The thieves take advantage of this situation.

52 *Yawm al-Tarwiya,* "the day of watering": The eighth pilgrimage day, just before arriving at 'Arafa from Mecca. Because Mina had no water, the Muslims provided themselves with water from Mecca before embarking

on the trip to Mina.

53 He is speaking here of the Islamic calendar.

54 In Islamic countries it is customary to wish that God accept the prayer or the pilgrimage of the addressee. Beggars take advantage of this and there is an allusion in their expressed wishes which links charity to God's greater acceptance of their performed duties.

55 *Al-Fitr* Feast: The small feast after Ramadan, the month of fasting.

56 Al-Shatir Hasan: The clever, brave, and ever-young hero of many folk stories.

57 Al-Ta'if: The summer resort of Hijaz from medieval times; an old verse of poetry goes like this: "Ni 'ma winters in Mecca, but her summer is spent in al-Ta'if," meaning that she is well-off. The habit of spending summer in al-Ta'if is still alive in Saudi Arabia.

58 Quraish: The most prestigious tribe of Mecca. It is the Prophet's tribe and that of many dignitaries in Islamic history.

59 Quran, *Sura* 113, verse 5.

60 See note number 19.

61 Cf. note 4 above. It is clear that the *Ustadh* 'Umar wanted Muhaisin to name the boy either 'Umar after him or a derivative of the name such as 'Amir, 'Ammar, etc.

GLOSSARY

'Afareet: Plural of *afreet,* a demon.

'Amm: Literally "paternal uncle". However, the word is used either before a man's name when the speaker wants to show respect to the addressee, usually because of an age difference.

'Areeka: A kind of sweet made of flour and butter, prepared mostly in the south of Saudi Arabia, on especially happy occasions such as the morning of a wedding. It is made in big trays and is often sold at the grocer's. Almonds may be added to the dough.

Batasa: A kind of sweet made of sugar and flour. It is baked in the shape of round Syrian bread, hollow inside, but is a little thicker than Syrian bread and more brittle.

Bazan: Public fountain.

Dibyaza: A sweet, thick drink made especially on the day of the Ramadan feast at the end of the month-long fast. The main ingredients are dates or sheets of apricot soaked in water, with sugar and nuts added.

Diwan: A collection of poetry by one poet. It can also mean an anthology of poetry by several poets.

Faqeeha: The word derives from a religious term, *faqeeh,* given to a man who is versed in religious studies, *fiqh;* sometimes used simply for a Quranic school teacher. Here, the name must have been given to these women out of charity.

Al-Fatiha: The first *sura,* or chapter, of the Quran. The name means "opening." This short chapter, memorized by all Muslims, is recited on important occasions such as a marriage agreement, or on visiting a grave where it is read on behalf of the dead.

Hajj: The annual pilgrimage in Islam. It is the duty of every able Muslim to perform the pilgrimage at least once in a lifetime. The pilgrimage season falls during the month Dhu al-Hijja of the Islamic calendar.

Halala: The smallest monetary unit in Saudi Arabia (a hundred *halala* equals one riyal).

Haram : This word, meaning "sanctuary," is given to the Kaaba in Mecca and to the Aqsa Mosque in Jerusalem, the two holiest shrines of Islam.

Al-Hareera: A kind of thick soup.

Hawqala: A Quranic verse said on difficult occasions to ward off the workings of the devil.

Igal: The headband worn over the *kufiyya*, or head kerchief, to keep it in place.

Jinn: Invisible beings, sometimes harmful but often helpful to human beings.

Jubba: A cloak worn as an overcoat and closed by buttons, similar to the one worn by Egyptian scholars.

Karabash: A plant ointment imported to the Peninsula from Southeast Asia, particularly from Indonesia, and used to cure illnesses or pain.

Khullaif: Those who tarry behind, i.e. the Meccans, mostly women and children, who, for some reason, do not join the pilgrimage.

Kuttab: An early Quranic school run usually by a single instructor (a woman for girls) which was popular in Arab countries before the establishment of public schools. The pupils were usually taught very elementary reading and the *'Amma,* part of the Quran.

Al-Mafatta: A large, usually round straw mat on which food is placed.

Majidi Riyal: A silver monetary unit from Ottoman times. "Majidi" is in reference to the Ottoman Sultan, Abd al-Majid.

Maqliyya: Known as *tu'miyya* in Egypt and *falafil* in Palestine, Syria and Lebanon: savory cakes made from pounded dry fava beans (soaked overnight in water) and other ingredients (sometimes mixed with pounded chickpeas), and fried in oil.

Al-Masha'ir: Holy places in the pilgrimage: Mina, al-Muzadalifa (where the pilgrims collect stones to throw on the devil), and Mount 'Arafa.

Ma'shara: round or sometimes rectangular trays piled with sweets and dates, usually covered with a light cloth. They are carried on the head, especially in the wedding procession which takes the bridegroom to the house of his bride. They are usually covered with a light cloth.

Ma'sub: A sweet delicacy made of wheat bread cut in cubes and put in special wooden dishes to which bananas are added and the two ingredients pounded together. Then sugar and goat butter are added.

Mawlana: A title of reverence and respect used for dignitaries, particularly learned men.

Mishlah: A loose cloak, often with golden threads on the fringes, worn loosely over clothing.

Mu'adhdhin: The man who calls the Muslims to prayer, usually from a minaret.

Al-Mutabbaq: A kind of pastry made of a thin dough folded more than once. It can be a savory or a sweet dish, stuffed either with ground meat, eggs and vegetables, or with bananas, eggs and sugar, or with sweet cheese or thick cream.

Muzahhid: The word is derived from *zuhd*, which means renunciation or indifference to worldly things. It can also mean "asceticism." The *muzahhid* is the person who calls on people to renounce their interest in worldly pleasures and possessions for the higher goal of worship.

Qaseeda: An ode. The old Arabic *qaseeda* was made up of equal verses, each composed of two almost equal hemistichs, with a monorhyme running through the whole ode, which could be of considerable length.

Qilada: Dried dates threaded together to form a kind of necklace.

Qubba: A dome, here, the highest class in school.

Rabat: A lodging for students seeking religious knowledge. It is used as a free hostel by people of certain nationalities, and should not be confused with the *rabat* used in military terminology to denote a garrison post.

Raushan: Protruding latticed windows, usually large, which allow women to look out without being seen from the outside.

Saqifat al-Safa: A small place situated at the end of the Abu Qubais Mountain in Mecca and part of the Ajyad quarter where the main character of the novel, Muhaisin al-Baliy, lived. The word *saqifa* means a covered place. *Saqifas* were areas covered with wood and palm fronds where people could take shade from the heat of the sun.

Al-Sayyid: "The master," a man excelling in something, here in folk remedies.

Sayyiduna: This refers to the fourth Caliph, 'Ali ibn Abi Talib, the cousin and son-in-law of the Prophet. After his assassination the Muslims split into Sunni and Shi'a, the latter being followers of 'Ali. *Sayyiduna* means "our master."

Shaikh: The basic meaning of this word is "old man," but it became, under special circumstances, a title of deference and eminence of status used in the Gulf countries in particular, even for princes regardless of their age. However, in the Arab world at large, it is mainly used for men knowledgeable in religious studies, or for teachers in traditional schools or *kuttabs*.

Showhat: A long, thin staff which teachers used on their pupils in the *kuttabs* and schools.

Shugduf: A kind of sedan, camel litter, houdah.

Sobya: A sweet drink especially popular in the fasting month of Ramadan because it satiates thirst. It is prepared by soaking wheat bread in water for some time, probably two days, and then adding sugar.

Sufi: An Islamic mystic.

Sura: A chapter in the Quran.

Taqiyya: A little hat worn on the head under the turban or other head gear or sometimes worn by itself.

Umm: Mother, or, when preceding a proper name, the mother of so and so. This is used to refer to married women in a respectful way and in order to avert calling them by their first names. For example, "Umm Hasan" means "the mother of Hasan."

'Umra: The minor pilgrimage which can be made at any time of the year and involves fewer ceremonies.

Ustadh: Means teacher, professor, or simply a word denoting a learned man (f. *Ustadha*).

Zar: A ceremony of African origin for exorcising demons which are believed to cause illness, disease, or psychological problems. The medium is usually a black woman. This practice is now prohibited in Saudi Arabia under the Saudi government.